DEATH AND THE CRONE

— *Top-Shelf Edition* —

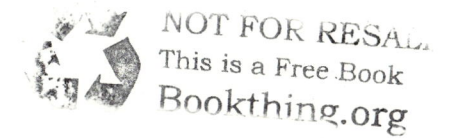

UPCOMING ESPEC BOOKS TITLES
BY MEGAN MACKIE

THE LUCKY DEVIL SERIES
The Finder of the Lucky Devil
The Saint of Liars
The Devil's Day

SAINT CODE
The Lost
Constable

MEGAN MACKIE

DEATH AND THE CRONE
— *Top-Shelf Edition* —

eBooks
PENNSVILLE, NJ

PUBLISHED BY
eSpec Books LLC
Danielle McPhail,
Publisher
PO Box 242,
Pennsville, New Jersey 08070
www.especbooks.com

Copyright © 2019 Megan Mackie

ISBN: 978-1-949691-29-0
ISBN (ebook): 978-1-949691-28-3

Published in an earlier edition by Mystique Press, an imprint of Crossroad Press.

All rights reserved. No part of the contents of this book may be reproduced or transmitted in any form or by any means without the written permission of the publisher.

All persons, places, and events in this book are fictitious and any resemblance to actual persons, places, or events is purely coincidental.

Copy Editor: Greg Schauer
Interior Design: Danielle McPhail,
Sidhe na Daire Multimedia
www.sidhenadaire.com

Interior Graphic: Mike McPhail, McP Digital Graphics
Cover Art and Design: J. Caleb Clark, jcalebdesign.com
Cover Element: https://depositphotos.com
         Middle-Age Woman © photography33

TO MY MOTHER, CONNIE, THE TEACHER.

"We all die. The goal isn't to live forever.
The goal is to create something that will."
—Chuck Palahniuk

CONTENTS

DEATH AND THE CRONE
1

EXCERPT:
THE FINDER OF THE LUCKY DEVIL
153

ABOUT THE AUTHOR
171

CHAPTER 1

THE YOUNG MAN UNLOCKED THE METAL DOOR AND LET IT SWING OPEN, beckoning Margaret inside. The old, homeless woman stopped on the threshold, a small wizened thing, wearing clothes that were never hers and stinking to high heaven of her own and others' filth.

"You are one crazy kid, you know that?" she told the young man standing before her, as he struggled a moment to remove the high-tech key card that never-quite-fit-the-lock from the door.

The young man flashed his youthful smile at her, tossing his newly freed keys and his umbrella onto the glass coffee table in the open living room. Without a further response, he walked past the island—the only thing separating the kitchen from the living room—to a refrigerator that shone dull silver in the dim light. The old woman stood still in the doorway, clinging onto the frame fighting her instincts to run. The room would have been less scary if it was filled with torture equipment.

Instead, a dark-wood dining room set with tall, throne-like chairs stood just a few feet from the doorway. To her left was a dark, leather couch with a clear, glass coffee table. Both pieces of furniture faced a wide flat-screen TV mounted on the wall. The couch sat on a beige carpet while the dining room set sat on wide square blocks of smooth stone-like tile with no wall in between to separate the two rooms like a sane person would expect. It was pure, uncomfortable luxury.

The extreme contrast of herself to the world in which she now stood, was so keen even she was embarrassed by it. The feeling penetrated through the hardened shell that told the world she didn't care what it thought of her, to touch the gentle, little girl she had once been, and in some ways still was, underneath.

"Come in, shut the door," the kid said from the kitchen.

Two glasses now sat on the island counter. She watched as he drew a bottle of something from his stainless steel fridge and set it next to them. Three red-topped stools waited on the opposite side for some glamorous woman in a too-short little black dress and heels to sit upon one of them. Not a woman dressed in rags, old enough to be his grandmother.

When she didn't move, he left the kitchen to come to her once more. He smiled his gentle smile, the one that persuaded her to take him up on his offer in the first damn place. As the smile washed over her, it made her insides melt. Most people shunned her at first sight, tried to keep upwind and at least five feet away—more if possible. It had been like that for too many years. This kid, instead, had come up to less than a foot beside her, both in the alley and now as she hovered in his doorway. Gently, he touched her shoulder to guide her inside and shut the door behind her.

"Would you like some water?" he asked. As he locked the door behind her, the old woman filled with a sense of doomed finality. Her skin itched.

"Whatever," she answered and proceeded further inside. If he didn't care about the crud on her tattered shoes staining his pretty carpet, then she didn't give a rat's ass either.

She brought her old body up onto one of the stools, though it took all her limited strength to climb up the damn things. It seemed to satisfy him, and he continued with that angelic smile as he poured out two glasses of bubbly water from the fancy bottle. While he did that, she studied him again in the light coming down from the three hanging lamps over the island counter.

He was beautiful. Too beautiful in her mind. Tall and thin without being gangly. The word 'lithe' floated through her mind.

He wore dark clothes, a fine black button-up shirt that was open at the top, and matching black slacks with dark, square-toed shoes she had seen models wear in magazines. His hair was the longish-style that only beautiful men could pull off without it looking like a mullet. The hair itself was dark, framing a perfectly chiseled face with nice cheekbones and a sharp chin. His eyes were dark blue, so dark the pupils were hard to see. They were as equally hypnotic as his smile. To her, they seemed like eyes that had seen too much, full of understanding instead of judgment. He had long fingers that handled the bottle of water expertly and she imagined for a minute those hands wrapping around her throat, choking the life out of her while she got to gaze deep into those dark, dark eyes. She snorted at the image.

"Look, kid, I know this has to be a part of some ritual for you or something, but you don't have to play nice with me before you do whatever the fuck it is you plan on doing to me. I don't really give a damn anymore," she said, defensively.

"I understand," he said and slid the glass of water over to her on its own fancy-schmancy coaster made of cork. "Drink that up, we have all night and you'll need it."

"What is this bullshit?" she grumbled but picked up the water anyway and stared down into it. "Probably drugged anyway," she said. Before she could take a sip, he plucked it out of her hands with those long fingers and took a healthy gulp instead.

"What the fuck? You fucking with me?" she snapped. "Some sort of power trip, you ass..."

"See, not drugged," he said and held it back out to her to take. She eyed him and the glass with hateful suspicion for several long minutes. The last thing she wanted was to reach out for it and be made a fool again. She had known several so-called men who would have thought yanking it out of her grasp the height of hilarity.

"I reach for that you will just snatch it back again," she concluded bitterly.

Nodding again with those damn understanding eyes, he set the water back on its coaster and picked up his own to drink. He leaned against the far counter, putting himself out of snatching range and watched to see what she would do.

She ignored the water. "Don't like feeling like a goddamn lab rat," she grumbled again. "You've got me up here, kid. Now, what do you want with an old bitch like me?"

"I told you, I'm interested in you. I want to help you," he answered and sipped his water, his eyes roving over her being.

God knows what he could be looking at. The old woman stared down at her wrinkled, scarred hands; the skin had gone thin until her bones showed underneath. She hated looking at her hands; she never recognized them. Over most of her body, she wore an old, burnt-orange jacket that was made for a man three times her size and went down to her knees. She liked it because it kept her warm on cold nights like this one if she tucked her knees into it. Dirty, white sneakers that were falling apart held her feet. On her legs were three pairs of sweatpants layered one over the other. She had just as many layers of shirt under the jacket, and her mess of gray, dirty, greasy hair was stuffed up under an old, black, knitted hat that she hadn't taken off for a long, long while. It was probably fused to her head by now. She hadn't seen herself in a mirror in years. She didn't have to. God knew how bad and ugly and old she looked, and this dumb fool just kept smiling at her as if she was... she was... what?

"What the fuck are you looking at, you freak?" she snapped again, with the old reliable defensiveness that was meant to keep her safe and away from harm.

He laughed out loud. Genuinely laughed, as if she had just told the world's greatest joke. There was no malice in it, which left her stunned.

"I'm looking at you, of course," he said, in that cryptic way that he had been doing for the last hour. Never quite answering her questions. He had picked her up in the alley only a few streets away. She had been digging through a garbage can when he came up beside her, an umbrella over his head to keep the light, cold drizzle of late fall from coming down onto his beautiful self.

"You want to come home with me?" he had asked after he had stared at her for a too-long moment. She was hurting, hurting for another fix or another drink, anything to keep the demons away. The need was so great that her instinct to protect herself gave way to the addiction, much as it had most of the years of her adult life.

She would have followed Lucifer himself if he had come a-calling.

"Why am I here?" she finally asked when the silence between them became annoying. Her skin crawled.

"Why do you think you are here?" he asked back.

"Because you either want to fuck an old cunt because you're sick in the head or something, or you want to murder me in some horrible way because who would miss street trash? So, whichever it's going to be, can we just get on with it?!" she shouted and swiped the glass of water off the counter. It made a satisfying, wet crash on the floor. "Because it don't much matter to me either way. I'm done with living."

He didn't move when she threw away his hospitality water. Didn't get angry either; just studied her, then slid his own glass of water across the counter to replace the one she broke and waited. She shot him an angry, black look, then picked it up. For a moment, she almost threw it after the other. It would have been satisfying, but she didn't. This time she stared at the crystal-clear liquid with its tiny bubbles and started to drink it. It actually tasted so good in her dry mouth. She couldn't remember the last time she had simply drunk water. As she gulped it down, she had to resist the urge to slosh it all over her face as well.

"How old are you?" he asked after she came up for air.

"Too damn old. Should have died years ago," she answered.

"Especially after all of the drugs you've done," he stated simply. Again, no judgment. Just facts. She still reacted as if he was judging her anyway.

"You been spying on me, you fucking animal?"

He held up his right hand, letting the sleeve fall back to show his right wrist. He tapped the wrist with the finger of his left hand and pointed at her own.

"You've got scars. I bet they go all the way up, don't they?" he said.

"Everyone's got fucking scars." She drank the last dregs of the water. It tasted so good, she didn't realize it was gone until she had tried to keep drinking when all that was left was air.

"Do you like doing it?" he asked. He retrieved the glass after she set it down and refilled it, emptying the bottle.

"What? Drugs? No. Who the fuck does? But the demon's gotta be fed. I owe him that much," she answered. "What's with the questions?"

"What demon?"

"What?"

"You said 'the demon's gotta be fed, you owe him.' Owe him for what?"

She set the glass gently onto the counter, becoming hyper-aware of the shake in her hands, her eyes drifting away to the other place. The place long in the past, the place where the demon had made its home and cried with a baby's voice. "I owe him for keeping the pain away."

The young man honored the silence around that truth. The creeping feeling in her skin that had been slowly building was impossible to ignore now. It was coming for her. Eating her alive, piece by piece. She'd waited too long. It would come for her and eat her heart. It would leave her dead soon enough. She needed the next fix to ward it off. The idea of her heart stopping, her life ending in writhing pain made her shudder. She had seen it before. Dying of withdrawal... even the corpses looked as if they were in agony.

While she didn't care if she lived, that wasn't what she wanted. Why wouldn't he simply end this already? It was becoming too hard to focus on him. The light was blinking in and out as she tried to stare at him with his hands braced on the counter behind him, his dark hair and dark clothes made out of the flashing darkness. She could see him for what he was now. The demon himself. He had come for her at last. He was beautiful.

"Come, it's time to take a shower," he said suddenly, straightening up to move around the counter.

"Shower?" she asked, blinking as she tried to bring awareness back to herself. The darkness melted off of him. Panic rose in her. A small voice said she should run now, but why bother? She came here to die by this monster's hand. She was going to do just that.

He took her wrist in his hand and pulled her off the stool to her feet.

"It's through here. Follow me, my beautiful girl." He led the way to a doorway just past the living room.

"I should just fucking run out the door right now," the old woman mumbled to herself, her old bones creaking as she moved. The right knee took its time working properly and she limped a few steps before it started smoothing out into a normal gait. He didn't comment or rush her. He was a well-mannered monster, she'd give him that.

He led her into a bedroom. It was much like the living room, in that it had the beige carpet and high-end motif. A king-size bed dominated the room, neatly made with a black comforter and heaps of pillows. A large mirror hung over the black wood headboard. Out of habit, the old woman side-stepped so she couldn't see her reflection. Again, the young man didn't comment, just led her to the right, through another entryway. He slid up a light switch to halfway as he passed, not that she could really see it. What she did see was the darkness of a ritual room, lit with fire all around. She didn't stop but double-blinked. The room changed as her demon—or was it a monster?—stopped and let go of her.

It was a bathroom, not a ritual room.

"A bathroom makes sense," she muttered. If he was going to kill her, bathrooms were easier to clean up.

"You're going to get clean in here." He reached into the shower—its own little room made of clear glass—and turned the water on. The rain shower head spouted water down, quickly filling the space with steam as the water made gentle plinking sounds on the faux-stone tiles. The young man shut the glass-door and turned to her, still smiling that goddamn peaceful, beautiful smile. Then he came up to her and started popping the snaps on the orange coat.

She jumped and flinched back, trying to bat his hands away, but her own shook so hard they had become useless. "What the fuck are you doing?"

"Undressing you," he said simply.

"I can do it myself." But she couldn't, her fingers wouldn't cooperate. "You want me to shower, right?" she asked, embarrassed. It wasn't a question she wanted answered, and he didn't answer it but simply waited. After a few moments, she gave up and he took over. "I gotta get all clean for you," she continued to mutter. Staring down at the ground, she realized the floor writhed beneath her shoes. She tried to look elsewhere, only to return her focus to the floor. It was better than looking at the walls as the monsters tried to push their way through the flames burning there. She felt like the small girl she hadn't been in years. Too late, those old memories surfaced once more, and she was twelve again, not innocent enough to not know what was coming.

"You need to get clean, yes. Come on, you'll feel better. Take ten years off of you," the beautiful demon quipped, and he reached out to pop more snaps. She stood there and let him, not moving or responding as he undid the coat and drew it off her arms. The smell got worse even to her blinded senses.

"It's...it's been a long time," she said in a small, shy voice, though whether she meant bathing or sex, she wasn't sure. Both were true.

"It's okay. Here, I'll dim the lights down even more so it's more relaxing." He moved to slide down the dimmer switch. Now they stood in a warm twilight serenaded by the gentle patter of water. The monsters growling in the ground and walls quieted as the light dimmed.

Patiently, almost like a nurse, he undressed her, one article of clothing at a time. As each piece came away, it was as if her skin was flayed off until she stood before this beautiful demon, her small, wrinkled, drooping body uncovered for his dark eyes to see. The lesions on her skin had gotten worse; scaly and red and sore. Gently with a thumb, he caressed one.

"Look at how beautiful you are," he whispered, and his fingers trailed up both arms to rest on her bare shoulders. She raised her head then, expecting to see craziness in his eyes or a mean quirk at the corner of his mouth. But his gaze remained just as loving as it had been. Her cheeks burned with an embarrassment she had thought life had pounded out of her years before.

"You're sick in the head," she said again, but she lacked the will to spit at him.

"Your life is all in your skin. Every wrinkle and crease. It's beautiful. You've lived so much," he said.

"It was a shitty life; I'm glad it's over," she said, gravelly. "My body's broken and useless."

"The most beautiful things are often broken. And besides, *you* are not your body. *You* are beautiful."

She blinked at that. "What? Am I already dead and this is heaven or something? Heaven's got a beautiful man waiting for me?"

That drew another one of his musical laughs, which made him look just a little bit crazy this time. She found his madness oddly comforting. At last, something she expected. "You'll have to tell me," he said and began to unbutton his own shirt.

She took a step back. "What are you doing?!"

Each button came away, popping one at a time to reveal a beautiful, well-muscled chest. His torso was long, and the edges of him were perfect. He toed off his shoes as he undid his belt in that way that every woman from the swooniest teen to an old crone like her recognized as sexy. "What are you doing?!"

"I'm going to bathe you. It'll be fine. I won't hurt you. I won't do anything you don't want. You have only to tell me," he said as he became beautifully naked himself. She stared at his long legs, which were just as muscled as the rest of him. He had to be one of those running fools that regularly shoved past her as they screamed at her to get out of the way, to get a pair of legs like that.

"No, no, this is wrong. This is wrong," she said as panic rippled through her. She wanted to run, but she was frozen to the spot as he approached in all his glory and pulled her into his arms, shushing gently in her ear.

"It's alright. I will take care of you. You are safe," he said and rocked her gently, so gently. He smelled good, like forest loam and summer rain and beautiful man. He smelled like a place and a person that she always dreamed would come for her, but never had.

What did she care? She came here to die.

"Do whatever you want," she whispered.

She let him draw her into the shower. He sat her on a stool waiting inside, and the warm water sluiced over her tired body. She thought it would burn her away, but after a few moments, the heat eased the cold inside her and she began to feel...truly warm. It had been a cold fall; frost and winter winds hounded the people of the streets earlier than they were ready for.

While he moved around behind her, she stared at her feet. The toes had been crushed inward ages ago, her toenails more like talons. Now they just looked like two old clubs at the end of deformed sticks. Between her feet, she watched the dirt swirl down the drain as the water washed over her. Grey foam replaced it as he began to lather over her back and arms. She went as compliant as a doll, her shaking easing somewhat. He left no cranny undiscovered or slathered in sweet-smelling soap.

"Jasmine?" she asked softly when he made a second pass.

"Do you like it?"

"Yes, it's lovely," she said as if in a dream. "It has been so long since I've felt so warm."

"Good."

A different soap, this one smelling of citrus, lathered up in her hair as his fingers slid through, finding tangle after encrusted tangle, but he never rushed and never stopped, breaking up the cakey mess with gentle fingers. He washed her hair four or five times, but by the last rinse, those long fingers rolled through the strands smoothly, gently massaging her scalp. She swore she fell asleep while he touched her, each pass a sweet caress, the likes of which she could never remember having felt before. The hypnosis lasted a long time. Letting the water continually wash over her, she realized he had stopped washing her and was simply holding her in his arms against his chest, skin to skin. At some point, he had shifted her back and off of the stool, but she had no memory of it. Her head rested on his shoulder, and he cradled her on his lap. It didn't feel strange or lewd. Instead, it was innocent and... sacred.

"How do you feel?" he asked softly.

"Oh, kill me now, because I cannot live after this," she sighed in pleasure.

"I was right."

"About what?"

"Took ten years off of you right there," he said, playfully.

"Oh, shut up," she snapped, the spell breaking. She tried to sit up, but he held her in place.

"Don't move just yet." He reached up above him to stop the water with a quick turn of the faucet. The old woman was sad it was over.

With ease, he stood up with her in his arms and carried her out of the bathroom and back into the bedroom. He laid her gently onto the bed, still wet, and pulled the clean sheet and comforter up and over, enveloping her in more delicious warmth.

"What is going to happen now?" she asked, watching his beautiful backside with its unbroken line as he went back to the bathroom, disappearing from sight.

"You will suffer," he answered. Her heart jumped in her chest, and she struggled to sit up.

"Fuck," she said. It was just as she feared, but her old body wouldn't respond, the ingrained aches that had been eased from the warm water still lurked beneath her skin. The walls and the covers of the bed rolled and fluttered once more. It made it so hard to sit up.

He returned from the bathroom carrying a bucket and several towels over one arm.

"Most likely, it will take several days," he continued, setting the things next to the bed. "I will keep you hydrated, but it will hurt, and there is nothing I can do about that." He pulled open a drawer in the nightstand next to the bed and pulled out long black straps, setting them on top before closing the drawer. "I might have to restrain you, but I'm hoping my holding you will be enough. Rest assured, I've done this before a few times. I'm going to try to make this as easy for you as possible."

The old woman tried to scramble away, to get out of the bed, and almost fell into the open maw reaching up to her from the other side of the bed. He was there then, her demon crossing the blackness as he tipped her back into the bed.

"Don't get up, it's already starting," he said. She tried to struggle—even though the room grew dimmer. She screamed in fear.

"Let me go! Let me go!!" she panicked. Something held her down, binding her in this hellscape that screamed and roared and laughed around her. Always that persistent laugh. Her whole body trembled so hard she barely realized she was crying. He shushed her gently in her ear.

"It's ok, it's ok. I'm here. I'll get you through it," he said.

She flinched, but he wasn't the demon. He was pure light with dark hair. He was there to save her. To ease her over to the other side.

"What? What the fuck have you done to me?" she hiccuped out. Then she understood, just before she passed out. The world faded away and melted into the old familiar pain.

"Your withdrawal has started," the demon's voice laughed from the edge of the bed, crawling across the sheets to devour her once more. Except he was already within her, always had been. Just before he raised his ugly head, his eyes black and burning, she thought about begging this other creature of light to kill her now. Then the demon pounced and took his price, chewing away at what was left of her—mind, body, and soul.

CHAPTER 2

THE OLD WOMAN STARED AT HER FACE IN THE MIRROR, HARDLY recognizing the being staring back at her.

"How long has it been since you've seen your own reflection?" the young man asked, his beautiful dark form standing behind her like a shadow in the dim light. Her eyes still ached as if the room was much brighter than it was, but at least she could stand any kind of light at all.

"Years. I hate mirrors," she said, and she leaned in a bit to study the wrinkled face before her. "I look like shit."

"You're beautiful," he countered, sounding amazed.

"Shut up. You said that to me when I was puking up all that shit you poured down my throat," she croaked, her voice sounding old even to her own ears.

"Water?" The mirth that filled his voice annoyed her.

"It burned like fire. Probably had something in it." She didn't believe that. Nothing ever tasted right when the demon was on her like that. Yet, she had never made it to the other side of withdrawal before, or at least not in too many years.

Now, as she looked at her face in the mirror, she tried to process what had happened to her since then. Her eyes were sunken into her face and there were hideously craggy wrinkles all around her eyes and mouth. She didn't dare linger on her ugly, browned teeth, closing her lips to hide them. Her hair, though it was clean and far whiter than she remembered, hung ragged around her face. There was no shape to it or any semblance of style. Just straight, flat, and white.

"I used to have waves in my hair," she said softly, picking at strands with her broken fingernails.

She stood there naked, but she definitely didn't care about that anymore. Her...new friend... captor...whatever...had seen everything her body could possibly do and hadn't run or dumped her in the nearest alley. That had left her strangely comfortable with the level of intimacy they currently shared as he watched her continue her examination, of which there was little left to discover.

Her ribs stuck out from under the dilapidated sacks that were once her breasts. Below that rounded the bulbous paunch of her belly. Below that...nothing else worth mentioning.

She shot a dark look at the young man standing behind her. "How can you call this beautiful?"

He shrugged and dropped a plain, cotton nightgown over her head, before helping to guide her hands into the sleeves. He had dressed in black jeans and a soft, white cotton t-shirt that just made him look sexier, his hair clubbed back in a small ponytail.

"You've gotten yourself through the worst of it. Now, it's just keeping you away from that stuff," he said, gently slipping the ends of her hair out of her collar. Everything he did was gentle.

"I'm sixty-eight years old, you dumb kid. What's the point?" she snapped as he pulled a hairbrush through her hair. She hated how much she loved the feel of him doing that.

"You're not dead yet," he said.

"I might as well be."

"Believe me, I'm just as surprised as you are."

"That I'm a still-walking corpse?"

"You're beauti...."

"Will you shut up!"

He laughed out loud as he set the hairbrush down and planted a kiss on top of her head, before turning to exit the bathroom. "Well...what would you like to eat? Do you feel like you can?"

"Do you realize that everything you are doing is absolutely useless? That once an addict...it's only a matter of time before I go out and use again?" she shouted after him. Her hip lanced pain down her leg as she tried to turn to follow him and she muttered curses under her breath. She was forced to lean against the sink waiting for the spasm to subside before trying again.

"Do you realize that ever since I brought you here you have done nothing but try to convince me how worthless you are, even though it is completely against your self-interest?" he shouted back.

"I'm a contrary, contemptuous bitch," she answered and paused between the bathroom and the entryway from the bedroom, winded. "And getting old sucks," she wheezed out as she grabbed the offending hip again.

"Do you need me to come get you?" he called.

"No, I'm coming," she answered stubbornly and pushed off again. He was busy in the kitchen, making clinking sounds as he worked. She focused on getting to a stool, but once she got there, she could hardly haul herself up.

"Why do these stools have to be so damn high?" she grumbled under her breath. Then his hands were behind her. Before she could shrug them off, he had boosted her up to sit smartly in the middle of the cushioned seat.

"I'm sorry I couldn't do more to help you. The stuff you were on was coated in half-baked magic to increase the potency. Any magical assistance would have...prolonged...things," he explained, planting his long arms on either side of her. He smelled so good. Granted, that was because he had just bathed her for the hundredth time since they met, but she still couldn't stop the pounding of her heart at the warmth of his chest against her back. Why was she letting this kid, this *child*, stir her up like that? She was a worthless, old has-been; a piece of trash ancient enough to be his grandmother, if she was being honest with herself.

"Would you rather sit at the table?" he asked softly.

"I'm fine," she muttered out of pure stubbornness, even though sitting at the table sounded better.

"As my lady wishes." He moved away to circle back around, depositing a plate in front of her.

"What the fuck is this?"

"Milk toast. It might be the easiest thing right now," he said as he French-pressed some coffee.

"Milk toast." She stared down at the plate of soppy bread, sprinkled lightly with cinnamon.

"Sister Agnes used to make that for me when I was a kid," he said and poured out coffee.

"You still are a kid," she shot back. "Sister Agnes? You were raised by nuns?"

"For a couple of years," he said. He continued putzing about in the kitchen, making his own milk toast and cleaning up his cooking mess while he ate.

"You should try this whole damsel-in-distress routine on some pretty young thing who's got something to offer you. It'd go over well," she said, taking a small bite of the milk toast with her fork.

"Nah, not interested," he said.

"For god's sake, why?"

"They don't know the songs," he answered cryptically, turning back to the fridge to pull out a clear glass jar filled with a syrupy, dark-red liquid.

"What the fuck is that?" she asked, staring at the jar as he unscrewed the top.

"The blood of virgins. It's supposed to be good for the skin," he said and poured some into his coffee. "Want some?"

The old woman bolted off the stool, almost falling over as she scrambled to get away. Panic slid across the young man's smiling face. "What's wrong?" he asked, rushing around the counter.

"You're a vampire?!" she shouted and held her hands up to ward him off, even though such an action would be completely useless against a bloodsucker.

He stopped mid-way to her, his dark eyebrows getting lost in his hair as surprise took its turn on his face. "A what?"

"You drink blood!" she quivered.

"No! No, it was a joke! I apologize. Look. It's just strawberry syrup, see?" He reached back for the jar and held it out to her.

"It's homemade. I get it from a dame down at the farmers market. Here try it." She eyed the jar he held out to her with cock-eyed suspicion. "Taste."

"Strawberry syrup in coffee?" she asked, her voice cracking into a high pitch.

"Yeah. I got the idea from a...well, friend would be a strong word for him. An associate of mine. Saw him do it once, thought I would try it. It's good, really."

Just then, a buzzer sounded, eliciting another yelp from the old woman.

"Dammit," he muttered under his breath. He set the jar back on the counter and moved to the intercom, jabbing the button hard with one finger. "Yes?"

"It's me," a young girl's voice piped through the speaker.

"That's a bit vague," he responded. While he was turned away, the old woman shifted her weight against the counter, her hip raging at her for the sudden backward not-quite-fall she'd just had.

"Elias, goddammit, let me in. I need your help," the intercom cursed back.

The old woman fidgeted as he glanced over his shoulder at her, his eyes looking a bit worried. "Now's not really a good time."

"Armageddon doesn't exactly care if it's a good time or not."

With a sigh, he hung his head a bit, then hit the button again. "I'll be right down," and he hit another button that buzzed harshly.

"Is that your girlfriend?" the old woman asked, entirely unamused by his attempt at a reassuring smile.

"No, a business associate, and it's always Armageddon with her. Don't worry, I'll be right back." He went over to a set of bookcases on the other side of his extra-wide dining room. To her surprise, he stuck his hand into the side of one shelf and pulled the whole thing away easily. A light flickered on as he opened the secret door. The bookshelf swung in to reveal a staircase leading down. "Just wait here, I'll be right back."

"So, your name is Elias, huh?" she asked.

He turned back to smile at her.

"You should eat your milk toast, Margaret," he said, before disappearing down the steps.

She stared at the open secret door for several minutes as her brain processed what it just heard. How did he know her name? It was strange that they hadn't exchanged names prior to this, but at the time she hadn't really given a rat's ass. About his name or anything else. She shouldn't even be sitting here.

Glancing down at the abandoned jar of supposed strawberry syrup, she dipped a finger in and scraped the liquid across her tongue. Her mouth burst with sweet strawberry flavor. "Elias," she said softly, savoring the taste of the words in her mouth.

"Hm," she grunted. "Stupid kid."

She wiped her wet finger against the side of the nightgown and looked toward the open secret door. "Nobody has a secret door without wanting to hide something."

She hobbled over and peered down the steps. There was another door at the bottom, also left partly open, like an invitation. The stairs themselves were made of black metal with narrow latticed steps. They reminded Margaret of something one would find in an old passenger ship. Voices drifted up the stairwell, too faint to hear.

Gripping hard onto the thin, metal rail, she lowered herself down one step at a time, slowly, her hip complaining the whole way. The room came into view through the open door near the bottom. She couldn't believe her eyes and stopped before she reached the last step. It was the most incredible shop she had ever seen in her life. As if in a trance, she continued down to stand in the doorway.

The place smelled of herbs and some combination of medical facility and old library. There were shelves everywhere filled with strange baskets and jars that reminded her of a co-op food store, except she couldn't readily identify most of what was on the shelves, and she saw no clear labeling system. Other than the herbs, strange objects like animals' bones and carved figures were displayed, resting on random tables throughout, giving the shop the chaotic topography of a curio shop. Across the room were two wide glass windows, set up with knick-knacky displays. The glass door between them had a bell hung above it. Streetlight poured in through the windows, the night coming earlier and earlier as fall marched to winter. The only other light hung over a counter along the left side nearer to the back. More small, exotic items festooned the counter. Sitting to one side was an old-fashioned cash register that would have fit in any five-and-dime store from her childhood a half-century ago.

Elias stood behind the counter next to a wildly spinning machine, his hands shoved into the pockets of his pants as he talked to an equally young woman with a head full of dreads. Three other people wandered around the shop. They all looked tough, street thuggish, to Margaret, except maybe the one near the bookshelves that lined the far-right side of the shop. She looked like a librarian, in her tan skirt, conservative sweater, and long, wavy, dark-blonde hair, frizzing on such a damp night. With careful deliberation, the young woman drew book after book from off the shelf, stacked them in a small pile, and then put every third book back with clear reluctance. Margaret hated her on sight. Life was so easy for that type: good little girls who never made any mistakes and always did what their mothers told them because their mothers hadn't been crazy.

"Margaret? Are you alright?" Elias asked, cutting off his conversation with the girl at the counter.

The girl looked over at her with an expression Margaret more easily recognized. It was a tough look, one made hard sooner than a kid should have had to be. That tough edge simply made her young freshness prettier and more striking. The old woman watched the girl look her up and down, with the same assessing attitude Margaret had come to expect: a large amount of judgment with a veneer of contempt.

"Who's this, Elias? Your grandmother?" she asked, her eyes narrowing as she met Margaret's angry gaze.

"That's none of your business, you little bitch," Margaret snapped before Elias could respond.

Elias chuckled at her response. "I don't know who she's going to be to me yet. She hasn't told me. I'm hoping it's true love."

"God, Elias, I didn't know you were a grave robber," the young burly boy piped in as he came to stand next to the tough girl.

Elias's smile phased from congenial to sharper at the edges. "There's much you don't know, about life or about me, kid. Grave robbing is the least of my crimes."

The boy shifted on his too-large feet. "Geez, man, that's not what I meant..."

"Crusher, just shut up," the tough girl snapped.

The little librarian finally came to the counter with her stack. "Thank you for opening up your shop for us, Elias. We really appreciate this," she said in an obvious attempt to smooth over her companions' conduct.

The machine next to Elias stopped spinning and beeped a piercing tone. He opened the top and pulled up two vials of some brownish liquid. With a quick twist, he capped them.

"Now, take this one before." He started to hand one vial to the tough girl but then stopped, turning it toward the light to study the liquid. He shook the vial and, within the brownish liquid, a glint of gold flashed. It was so bright that Margaret could even see it from the doorway. Everyone leaned in to try to make out whatever it was, blocking her view. She left the doorway and hobbled over to the counter for a better look. "Yes, this one, take the one with the green stopper first. Blue stopper is for after. Don't mix them up."

The tough girl slipped one of her dreads behind her ear only for it to fall back against her face again. "What happens if I mix them up?"

"If you don't take the green one first, you'll probably go mad, and if you don't take the blue one second, you're going to be really constipated for three days from taking the first one. I highly recommend taking them in the right order, green then blue." Eyes wide, she nodded and took the vials, tucking one into each pouch in the front of her combat belt.

"Got it, great," she said dryly, then shouted over her shoulder, "Are we ready, crew?"

The librarian moved to the center, having settled on three books out of her whole stack, the rest left abandoned on the opposite end of the counter. The other of this group, a wiry Lionman that looked too thin for his clothes and a bit ridiculous in all the studded leather he wore—never mind the braids in his mane—emerged from the shelves carrying two jars. Elias eyed the items as they set them on the counter then hit some buttons with one finger on the register, putting his other hand back into his pocket as he did so.

"Let's call it $3,000 even," he said.

The kid called Crusher made a choking noise, but the tough girl didn't bat an eye. She reached into another pouch on her belt and pulled out a wad of bills that she flipped into her hand and counted, before handing half of the stack to Elias. He didn't even look at it, just pushed it into the register and shut the drawer. That's when Margaret felt that thrum of off-ness that sometimes came out of nowhere. Most of her life, she just ignored it, but at that moment, she knew clearly that it had come from the cash register.

"Thanks for your business. Good luck with everything," Elias said politely, but it was also an obvious dismissal.

"Yeah, thanks again," the tough girl said, then glanced again at Margaret with a blank expression.

Elias set a hand on Margaret's far shoulder and pulled her around the counter to his side. She stumbled a little as she came up against him. He squeezed gently as if to reassure her of something. The whole group flinched and exchanged looks of barely veiled discomfort. As they left, they shot her various looks of contempt, confusion, and disgust at his familiar gesture. They were probably all wondering what was wrong with him. Margaret wondered the same thing herself. She wanted to pull away and snarl, but Elias's stronger grip held her tight, and her hip hurt too much to really try.

Once the last kid passed through the door, Elias let her go to follow them and locked up.

"So, what do you think?" he asked, turning back to her.

"Of what?"

"My shop?" He gestured at the room.

"What kind of shop is it?"

"Mostly a this-and-that sort of place. I got a little bit of everything here, and I can usually find most anything else that my clients might need," he said, walking back toward her.

"You're a pain in my ass," Margaret snapped at him.

"Why is that?" he asked, still unreasonably unperturbed by her anger.

"You don't answer a single damn question straight," she growled.

He nodded at that. "My cousin says the same thing. That's been my way for a long time. I suppose it frightens you, that you don't know why you're here or what my intentions are," he said more to himself, rather than asking her. He ran a hand through his hair and ended by tugging on his ear. Margaret blinked at the obviously nervous gesture. "Ha. This is...this is surprisingly difficult. Once it looked like you were going to live...I've had all week to figure out what I wanted to say to you, but now the moment's here and I've got butterflies."

"Just say it, you stupid kid." Margaret was at the end of her rope with all of this and was ready to start smashing things if it meant she might get a straight answer. She came back from around the counter, leaning on the end to ease her hip.

"Well, I've decided I like you," he said. There was a heavy silence as Margaret waited for him to say more.

"What the fuck are you talking about?"

"Exactly what I said, I...I like you. I have a unique attraction to you that I don't fully understand yet, and I would very much like to explore it. I want you to stay with me...and let's actually get to know each other," he said, his cheeks blushing. It was the first time Margaret had seen more out of him other than that cool, detached but friendly calm. Yet, she could only note the shift in him as her brain exploded.

"What the fuck do you mean? You like me? I'm old, you dumb shit! I am an old woman, and you are... You should be with a..." Her heart pounded, but along with the familiar rage, there was also a tremor of...excitement? "What the hell is wrong with you? You must be sick in the head?!"

"So you keep shouting at me," Elias answered, finally a little terse, and he walked past her to go back around the counter, his shoulders and movements stiffening with agitation, as if he was upset by what she just said. Well, good. Someone needed to straighten the dumb kid out.

"You're just after some old pussy then? Go hit up an old folks' home. You'd have better luck there than with an old poxy whore like me."

"You really hate yourself, don't you?" he asked, stopping her rant cold.

It was the truth and it hurt to hear. Margaret gripped the counter and just stared at Elias, unable to move or breathe.

"If you wanted to fuck me, why haven't you already?" she growled out.

The tiny, youthful crinkle returned to the corners of his eyes.

"It's interesting that you assumed that was part of the deal."

That stopped her in her proverbial tracks. He was right; she did assume he was after one of two things. Yet, she stood there both alive and, as far as she knew, untouched. She blushed as the reliable feelings of shame boiled up. Forcing herself to convey dignity, she puffed up her chest.

"And what about now? Or maybe I should just leave. Get out of here." It wasn't really a threat, so why did it feel like one?

"I don't want you to leave."

"Then what do you want from me?!" Her voice filled the shop, so loud that even she winced at the sound. Why wouldn't he give her a straight answer?

"I want you to eat milk toast and talk to me," he said softly.

"This is ridiculous. No one cares about a useless old woman," she said, repeating her thoughts out loud. "This is a fucking folktale."

That brought out his laugh. "Yes, I suppose it is."

"Ugh! There is no talking to you!" She turned to leave. Maybe to go upstairs and get dressed in…something. She needed to get out of this uncomfortable situation.

"What do you think Death and the Crone do while the heroes are off hero-ing?" That stopped her, and she turned back to him. "Do you think they sit around and wait, or maybe they have their own folktale adventure? What do you think?"

"Death?" Margaret asked, arching an eyebrow at him.

Elias gave a Cheshire-Cat grin.

"Folktales are overrated," she answered. "And if this was a folktale…this kind of thing, being rescued like this, only happens to the beautiful young girl that has something to give," she said, lifting her head to meet his eyes straight on. "You're decades too late. So, why now? Why is my knight-in-shining-armor here now, when I am like this?"

That drew him from out behind his counter. "I told you, I'm a wizard, not a knight-in-shining-armor. I like it better.

Fewer rules regarding wizards, other than that we need to be eccentric."

Margaret blinked. "Wait. What are you saying? You are a wizard, or you're Death?"

"Yes," he smirked.

She rolled her eyes, which ended with her looking up into his face as he approached. His eyes locked with hers with a hypnotic tension. Her heartbeat quickened and she could taste his breath as he exhaled slowly, the smell of coffee and strawberries.

"What are you doing?" she challenged when he passed the invisible social barrier that determined where 'too close' was.

He smirked. "What would happen, do you think, if I were to kiss the crone? Would she melt into a princess?"

"Ha, not likely!"

She didn't back away. She had no intention of giving this young pup the satisfaction of knowing his wiles were getting to her. She'd show him what a blushing virgin never could.

His fingers came up along the side of her face, cupping her cheek in a way no man had done in years. "Is there any harm in trying?"

"What if it does the opposite, and I suck the life out of you 'til you're a pile of bones?"

He leaned in any way. "If only." And kissed her.

It tasted like a memory. His lips caressed hers, warm and inviting, gentle but firm. He closed his eyes, even as hers widened at his touch. Feelings rippled through her, overwhelmed her, and her eyes softened before closing also, as she was carried away by the sensations. He had her so firmly entranced, she just gave in and let it happen. His lips moved, and she felt the tip of his tongue dart in just a little bit, hitting a spot on the other side of her upper lip that sent tingles across her skin to her toes. She moaned softly into his mouth and felt him smile as he broke the kiss, but kept his face close, touching her nose with his.

"Well? Did anything change?" he whispered.

She opened her eyes dreamily and looked up at him. What he said made no sense, but she didn't care. His eyes smiled at her and she believed, honestly believed that the smile was sincere and it was because of her.

"You're so beautiful," she said without realizing it.

"*You're* so beautiful," he insisted, "and you can't even see it. My gosh. I'm giddy. I'm genuinely shaking here." He backed away, breaking the contact.

That move broke the spell and she remembered herself as he let her go, putting some distance between them as if he needed it to stop himself. A small part of her wished he wouldn't, the part of her that had never aged, even as her body had against her will.

He passed a hand over his face. "Let's go upstairs. We should get you upstairs. You look pale as a ghost." Elias flipped off the light over the counter. "There's nothing more for us down here."

"And what is there for me upstairs?" she asked.

"Bed, I suppose. I'm tired," he said.

"The same bed?" Margaret asked.

His laugh, this time, was a bit nervous, making Margaret feel unsure. "Yes, the same bed. There is only one bed up there. It's been that way all week." Elias cleared his throat. Then he laid a hand on her back to steer her toward the steps.

"A week?"

"I suppose. You've been in and out of it this whole time, and I have not been sleeping on the couch." He brought her to the steps, but she stopped and glared at them.

"Can you not get up them?" he asked, noting her hesitancy.

She huffed. "I can," she said stubbornly, but when she moved to take the first step, her body betrayed her and she yelped.

"What's wrong?" he pressed.

"My hip is out," she grumbled.

"Which one?" he asked and laid his hands on both of her hips.

She tried to shake him off. "You're pretty damn handsy there, kid." Again, the hypocrisy of her statement was not lost on Margaret. She did just let him kiss her.

He pressed his thumbs in on either side of her hip bones and she yelped. "It's the right one, then?"

"Yes! You devil! Jesus that hurts," she shouted, grabbing the rail of the stairs before she passed out from the pain.

"Come on then, I'll carry you up. Maybe I can use a little magic to..." he said, but she slapped his hands away again.

"Don't touch me. I can get up myself," she said. Then she lost her balance and fell backward.

"Margaret! Are you alright?" Elias asked as he rushed to catch her, too late. No sounds came out of the old woman, as she lay at the foot of the stairs, her focus on trying to take the next breath. Her hip had given out and now throbbed lances of fire down her leg. For a moment, her vision blacked out, then melted back into color and shape.

"Stop! Stop pawing at me," she snapped, then stretched up her hand. "Just... just pull me up." His larger hand gripped one of hers, and his other caught her elbow while he came around to face her. With a steady pull, he leveraged her upright onto her feet. There was a loud and fundamental cracking sound.

"Ah!" she cried, and she grabbed onto the front of his shirt.

"What...where are you hurt?" Elias said, his voice rising higher in pitch as he panicked. "We should sit you down again."

"No, no. Wait. Wait," Margaret said as she shifted her hips gently from side to side. "There's no pain. Oh my god." She let go of his shirt and took an easy step back. The hip responded, but she felt no sharpness or even the ache that typically followed when she managed to get her hip back into its place. "There's no pain. There's nothing. I..."

She took a few more steps forward, moving easily. Her knee didn't hurt in response. Even the waddle she had had for the last ten years was gone. She walked and turned smooth, steady, and sure, like a woman several years younger than herself. "What..." She began to giggle uncontrollably. "I'm walking. Elias! Look, I'm walking. What...What did you do?"

"Nothing," he answered, looking pleased with himself anyway. "I haven't done anything."

Margaret's face dropped immediately. "Of course not, that's stupid. My hip just went in. Why am I getting all excited about that? That's stupid," she chided herself out loud.

"Must really feel good then," he said. She scowled at him, not that he noticed. "Ready to go upstairs?"

"Just shut up," she said and climbed the stairs all the way to the top, all by herself. She had to keep her face pointed straight ahead, so he didn't see her smile.

CHAPTER 3

THE NEXT MORNING, SHE WOKE TO THE SOUND OF SOMEONE IN THE kitchen. Her whole body felt stiff and clumsy like any other normal morning, but it was surprisingly easy to sit up. Looking around the room, it took a moment to recognize her surroundings. She was in his bed. His fine, supremely comfortable bed.

She had vague memories of the night before.

When they had come back up to his place from the shop below, she had found herself utterly exhausted. She wasn't sure she actually ate the milk toast he had made her, but he had herded her to his bed. From the way the pillows on the other side of her had been disturbed, she was pretty sure she hadn't slept alone. The hip continued to stay in place, even if the rest of her was still past its expiration date.

She sat there a moment, taking in her surroundings. What was she still doing here? He hadn't done her the favor of killing her, and if this was some kinky sex-thing it was a slow-burn one. There was no way this... abduction...seduction...whatever it was, could be what it seemed.

Yet...

In another life, several lives ago, she once entertained a fantasy of a beautiful, kind, young man sweeping her away and taking care of her in a beautiful house. A young man who would make all the bad memories go away. It was unsettling how close this came to that. Painfully close. But like she had said, it was decades too late, and she was long past deserving it, not with the sins on her soul.

"You're an old, used-up woman. No one wants you." Margaret paused in her ascent from the bed. The voice was faint and far away, but she heard it as clearly as if it whispered in her ear. *"You need to get out of here..."*

Then, somewhere in the next room, a bell chimed once. Feet clacked across the wood floor, and a door opened. Margaret heard muffled words, then the door shut again. Then silence.

Curiosity seemed to have awoken with her that morning. Intrigued, she pushed herself out of the bed and set her ugly feet to the beautiful, smooth, wood floor. Just as she cracked the door to take a little peek, Elias looked up from whatever he was doing in his little kitchen haven. Margaret cursed her bad luck as she had no choice but to leave the bedroom and be civilized.

"Good morning, Margaret," the dumb kid said, with way too much energy.

"Why are you so cheerful?" she growled at him, rubbing the side of her face, uncertain if what she felt were wrinkles or pressure marks. Not that she cared either way.

"Do you drink coffee?" he asked, dodging her question.

She pushed herself forward and waddled stiffly over to the counter where Elias set a black mug of the stuff in front of her without waiting for a real answer. Creamer and sugar waited in a bowl beside it, but she ignored them. This was not a morning for gentled coffee. She sipped at the pure dark stuff and had to suppress a moan of pleasure. No matter how bad things were in her life, at least she always had coffee to fortify her. It was the steady beacon of normalcy she could always count on, even here with the strange circumstances she found herself currently in. It was simply an added bonus that it was really, *really* good coffee.

Once most of the cup was gone, she looked toward the couch, noticing the boxes laid out there. She pursed her eyebrows together at them. Each was marked with a smile on the sides.

Sniffing contemptuously at the smug boxes, she turned away. At least that answered her question about who had been at the door.

"I have some toast here, but if you're up to it, I can make you something more substantial," Elias offered, pushing aside a newspaper he had been reading on the counter. He held his own coffee mug. It was a fancy, clear glass one and was maybe a quarter full. How long had he been awake? What time was it now?

Margaret exhaled a deep sigh. Okay, well, if he wanted to play house, she'd play house for now.

"Could I have…pancakes?" she asked. It was a childish request, especially since she wasn't really hungry, but the hominess of the idea appealed to her.

Elias brightened. "Coming right up," he said and set to work.

"A little more coffee, too," she barked out.

When the fresh pot of coffee appeared before her and refilled her mug, she wrapped her gnarled fingers around it, letting the warmth burn through her skin to her bones. The kid…*Elias* continued to clank around the kitchen, pulling ingredients and tools from various cupboards and assembling them with a chef's professional speed. Soon, an electric griddle hissed and spat as he poured out perfect circles with a ladle. Margaret watched silently, savoring her black coffee.

"I'm leaving this morning," she finally said as he waited with a spatula to flip the disks.

"How do you mean?" Flip, flip, flip, flip went the pancakes.

"Dammit, what I said." Margaret banged her coffee cup on the counter. "What exactly are you expecting me to do here? Just eat your food and take your kinky baths? And for how long?"

Elias blew out a hard breath. "Well, how long would you like?"

Not a question she could possibly begin to answer. "What are you looking for here? A kept girl?" Margaret shook her head at the thought.

He shrugged. "Well, bringing someone like you into my home; it's not like you're my prisoner or a sex slave or anything like that." He held up his hand to stop the words perched on her lips in response. "I enjoy your company, Margaret. Conversations with you are interesting. I bet you have plenty of compelling stories."

"Not at all. They're the same old stories that everyone has. What is there to tell about an old, used-up woman who never lived? Who wants to hear stories about that?"

"A sad and lonely person would." Something about those words rang truer than they should have. "Don't disregard the power of empathy."

"Empathy." Margaret took another sip. "I have no idea what empathy is. Just sounds like a four-dollar word someone wants to sell you for two. So now it's worth two. Like love."

"I can relate to that," Elias said, with a barely suppressed smirk.

Margaret narrowed her eyes as she realized what he had done. This boy was too smart for his own good. "If it's just empathy you want, then why the naked baths and sleeping in the same bed?"

"Hasty intimacy with very little consequence, with a woman who obviously knows what she's doing and what she wants," he replied, arching an eyebrow at her. "Doesn't that sound like fun?"

Margaret's traitorous cheeks went hot.

"That's a lot of talk for very little action. Unless something happened when I was out of it."

Elias paused and regarded her with warm eyes. "I'd like to say, of course not, but there's nothing 'of course' about that is there?"

A knot twisted in Margaret's stomach. "What?"

Elias put up his hands alarmed. "Oh, no. No! That's not what I mean. Nothing happened. I'm just saying that there must have been others who…"

"I know what you're saying," she cut him off.

"I wouldn't be averse to it," he said, recovering.

"Bah, you're full of shit. If you were going to knock heels, you would have already. You probably took one look at me and it all shriveled up, didn't it?"

Another chuckling laugh. "Not at all. You are sacred to me, Margaret."

"Shut up," she started, but it was cut off by the clink of a plate, now stacked with four perfect pancakes.

"I mean it. Your presence, your grace—"

"I'm ancient."

He barked his laugh this time as if he had been caught by surprise. Margaret narrowed her eyes. "What's so funny?"

"So is the Venus de Milo," he said, "or the Mona Lisa. People still say they are beautiful."

"They are unchanging."

Elias nodded as he checked the underside of the next batch of pancakes on the griddle. "And yet not. I do believe the Venus did have arms at one point." He eyed her as she poked at her pancakes with a fork. "Something wrong?"

"No butter? No syrup?"

The beautiful man started and turned back to the fridge. "Sorry, sorry. I got lost in your words."

Accepting the cold syrup, Margaret pursed her eyebrows together, pinching the worry line that was always there even deeper.

"Are you married, Margaret?" he asked spontaneously.

"Hell no! I don't need to marry some worthless man, who's barely off his mom's tit."

Elias laughed again. "I need to introduce you to my cousin. I think you'd like each other."

The old woman arched an eyebrow at him. "So, you *do* have family?"

"A cousin, yes. I mean, I have more family than that, but she's the only one I would ever put the word to. Maybe my uncle, but I'm still angry with him right now." He snapped off the griddle and came around the counter to sit on a stool next to Margaret. "And yes, there is a reason I chose someone from the street, for exactly the reason you're thinking; nobody will miss you, and nobody will interfere with us."

"Of course. You don't want anyone knowing your little, kinky secret. What? You plan to keep me locked up here so no one ever sees me again?"

He plated his own pancakes. "Except for the four kids I introduced you to downstairs yesterday?"

Oh, that's right. He did.

"Will you please stay?" he asked, setting his hand on hers.

"No," she said flatly. "As soon as we're done here, I'm gone. I don't need this charity of yours any longer. It's not who I am." That was bullshit, but he didn't know that. "...I had clothes before," she continued, stuffing a bite of pancake in her mouth. That stopped any further words as she rolled the buttery sweetness over her tongue. It hit her then, how long it had been since she had tasted anything that... well... tasted like anything.

"Good?" Elias asked, noticing her reaction.

Margaret looked away, the tears burning in her eyes. Why was she so weepy? It had been years since she had truly cried, why so much now? "It's fine." Now that she had put something in her mouth, her stomach informed her how hungry she really was. Without any restraint, she began to eat, shoving the food in as fast as she could manage to chew and swallow. Hungry! To be *hungry* again. It was like she had been a walking corpse. Now she was alive and hungry!

She almost didn't notice Elias set the rest of his untouched pancakes onto her plate and get up to fry up the last of the batter. When she had finished eating and sat contentedly with her coffee, she wondered if she would end up throwing up the food later. Her digestive system was being very compliant today.

"Would you like more?" Elias asked as he reached for her empty plate. She shook her head no, and he deposited the plate into a dishwasher.

He cleaned up the rest of his kitchen, restoring it to its pristine condition while snatching bites from his replaced pancakes as he went. Once he was done, and his own empty plate dropped into the dishwasher, he walked into his living room and dropped onto his couch. With an exaggerated groan, he propped his feet up on the table and sighed. His arms splayed across the back, which pulled his buttoned shirt up a little bit, flashing a bit of skin just below his navel. Leaning his head back, he closed his eyes and went completely quiet.

"Don't you need to open your shop?" Margaret asked, not even trying to hide the fact that she was staring.

"Nope."

"Why? Is it Sunday or something?" She turned away and stretched across the counter to grab the paper still folded up and abandoned there.

"I think it's Tuesday," he answered.

"So, is this what you do with your days? Sit around?" Margaret gave up on the paper. It was too far to reach anyway.

"I'm waiting," Elias sing-sang out petulantly.

She blinked at him. But he didn't continue. Instead, he laid there with his eyes closed. "For what?" she finally asked.

"For you to open your boxes." He indicated the line with the point of his toe, before lazily plopping it back on top of the other foot. He still hadn't opened his eyes. "I burned your other clothes in case you were wondering. I figured the least I owed you is some new ones."

Margaret double blinked. Looking at the boxes with new eyes, she counted them. There were six in total, stacked in a rough pyramid on the couch, each about two feet long.

Elias seemed to take in the shocked look on her face with delight, having finally opened his eyes to enjoy it. Getting up, he slipped a knife out of his pocket, snapping it into its useable form with a flick of his wrist. Margaret flinched back from the sound with a fearful startle. She had heard it too many times in her life.

Her host didn't seem to notice as he set the blade to the top of the closest box and sliced through the smooth tape. Tissue paper crinkled as he flipped back the cardboard flaps to reveal a soft sweater the color of peaches from inside. She stood there, staring.

"Go ahead, touch it. It's butter-soft," he said.

Still, she didn't move. He went still as her eyes flicked to the knife in his hand. Nonchalantly, Elias stepped away from the boxes containing the sweater and went to open up the others before closing the knife. Margaret watched his every move as he slowly walked across to the kitchen and closed the knife into one of the drawers. With great care, he returned to the boxes and pulled out various clothes, laying them all out for her in an array of colors. There were more sweaters and equally soft-looking shirts, along with a couple pairs of jeans stitched with elastic waistbands, and loose black yoga pants. Other necessaries were set out still in their packages waiting to be torn into. From the last box, he withdrew a coat. It was a long, winter coat, made of dark brown suede, the collar lined with something that seemed like dusted fur.

"Well?" he finally asked.

She knew what he wanted from her. He was looking for some approval. A pat on the head for the bounty he had just laid out before her as if it was no big deal. And she knew it really wasn't that big of a deal for someone like him. Yet, as she watched him lay out the clothes, her mind had calculated and assembled each complete outfit. A flash of faces burst through her mind, and she assigned an outfit to each of them. Who they would look good on, who could benefit from such generosity. However, as soon as her mind made those connections, old memories followed on their heels. That face was dead. That face was missing. That face would never speak to her again. That face was also dead. Over and over. So many gone. So many that she had known, who had survived with her on the street, banding together and breaking apart as needed. So many gone. So much of her life already spent. Time she would never get back, with choices she could never remake. Now that she was sober, she remembered why she drank and drugged and took chances, all to dull the enormity of these feelings. No one should have to live bearing the weight of such memories. Why did she still exist? True, she could have rushed to meet death easily enough, but she couldn't bring herself all the way to the final end. At the same time, she didn't run from it either. But death kept passing her by. Every OD, every close call she had survived while others had died. Even Death didn't want her, despite what the stupid kid claimed.

What was the damn point of it all?

Tears ran down her face hot and thick. It didn't really register that she was crying as she stared down at the various clothes that could have covered and warmed so many. So many who were gone. A tear for each memory burned down her craggy face, finding the riverbeds and streams that had not been filled in so long.

She didn't see him come before her. She didn't see much of anything. But suddenly, Elias was there, and if the tears felt like boiling hot water, his lips pressing to hers were fire.

His hands cradled her face and tilted her head just enough to accommodate his height, intensify his kiss. There was barely a breath between them. How could he stand it, to kiss a woman with awful teeth like hers, even if they were clean now? Even with his fancy toothpaste, they were so far gone and rotten, there was no way someone would find putting their mouth near hers an appealing thought. Her fingers wrapped around his wrists with some fleeting idea that she should push him away, yet the sweet pain of this kiss felt more right, like what she truly deserved, than anything else he had done so far.

Changing her grip, she ran her hands up through his hair, sinking her fingers into its softness and pulling him closer, slipping her tongue inside him to make it a real and proper kiss. He gasped slightly as she took control, before yielding, following her lead. She may have been an old, unworthy woman, but the one thing she knew: she was a talented kisser.

Margaret lost control of the situation as quickly as she had seized it. Elias swept her up from her feet, the nightgown she wore billowing like a white wing as he turned to take her to his bedroom. In any romance novel, the heroine's heart would have leapt, and Margaret's did, but not in a romantic sense.

"Put me down!" Margaret cawed, the minute she was tipped off her equilibrium.

"I will. In a moment..." Elias pushed the door open too hard with his foot, banging the wood against the wall in his eagerness to bring her to his bed.

"Be careful!" She tried to pull herself up higher on him, even as he tried to lay her down in the still rumpled sheets. She arched away like a cat trying to escape a bath.

Since gravity didn't care about what Margaret wanted, her antics only pulled them both into the bed as Elias lost his balance. His laugh complemented her screeches as they bounced on the mattress, him half-on, half-off her.

"Oh, sorry. Am I crushing you?" he asked with delayed concern. His breath seemed to catch as he gazed down at her face, now mere inches from his own. She knew he was going to lean in again, but when he did, he went to the side. He planted a light, sustained kiss at the corner of each of her eyes, before nuzzling her gently with the tip of his nose, curving along her cheek toward her ear. Margaret's inhale at the sensations caught in her throat as his mouth sought out the sensitive place between her ear and her neck. His fingers drifted down to hook the edge of her nightgown, slowly drawing it up.

I don't care, she told herself. Finally, this would be over, and she truly could get out of there, her debt to him, for all the food and the board, paid. It was his own fault if he wanted such cheap coin for it.

Chiding herself, she waited, letting him bring her nightgown to her hip, where he decided to stop. Oddly, she had the urge to push his hand away to stop further progression, but he had already seen her naked repeatedly, so what was the point? It wasn't as if she hadn't decided to let him do whatever he wanted with her. Still, something pulled sharply inside her heart.

"Stop," she squeaked.

He did immediately. That really surprised her. But he did. He removed his hand from her side and placed it on the pillow next to her head before lifting his face to look down at her, his eyebrows knitted in concern.

"What is it?" he asked softly.

She jerked her head to the side, her face going sullen once more.

"Margaret? What is it?"

"Nothing!" she snapped.

"Margaret?" He settled back again, regarding her. "This isn't crazy. This is natural..."

"Just do whatever it was you were going to do!" She put her arms up to increase his access to her body, but still, he didn't touch her. In fact, he did the opposite; he turned away so he could sit beside her, placing both feet back on the ground.

"Did I hurt you?"

"No."

Still, he didn't move. She wasn't going to break first, so she continued to lay there waiting for him to just get on with it. Instead, he stood up. Carefully, he drew the blankets back over her and left without another word.

Once the door closed, she turned over onto her side.

It was only a matter of time, now, before he threw her out. She cursed herself. This dream was obviously a too-good-to-be-true thing, but she did what she always did, hastened the inevitable end. No one could put up with a bitchy whore like her for long anyway.

CHAPTER 4

IN THE DARK, A BABY CRIES. A BABY THAT WILL NEVER BE BORN. THE demon is coming for her. The dark demon keeps the baby's cries at bay. Her suffering is the cost to shut the little, crying thing up. Margaret is always willing to pay that price, but she is reneging on that deal. Now, the dark demon beckons.

"You must come back, Margaret. You are not allowed to shut yourself away. We have a deal."

She has to get out of there.

Shaking from the nightmare, Margaret sat upright in bed, the only person in it. She had stayed away too long. She needed to get back onto the street where she belonged.

With greater reluctance than she thought she would feel, she pulled herself out of bed. But she had to leave. And now was the chance as she saw no sign of Elias. If she didn't get out now, the temptation to stay would be too great.

This wasn't where she belonged.

"Time to get the fuck out of here," she said out loud again as if trying to convince herself that this was what she had to do. She pushed herself to her feet and went to peek out the door. Elias was gone. The bookshelf leading down to his store stood ajar, so she had a fair guess where he had escaped to. If she moved quickly, she should have enough time to make her own escape. How much of the day had she slept? Why was she sleeping so much?

Her old clothes were gone. She wasn't attached to them or anything, but even she had enough dignity not to want to walk out into the street in just an old nightgown and bare feet.

That left her host's gift of clothes. They were presently in their boxes, waiting in the closet. She dived into them with no shame. They were for her anyway, so it wasn't really stealing.

From the first box, she fished out a Windy City t-shirt like one would find in a kitschy tourist shop and a liquidy soft sweater the color of rose petals. The next box held a packet of underwear and another of socks. From the bottom-most box, she retrieved a plain pair of jeans and a bra. She also found a new pair of white sneakers that actually fit her, even if they were a bit stiff. As she hurried to get dressed, she dashed away the painful tears in her eyes. Stupid clothes. She couldn't weep every time she saw them, she had to focus. The coat wasn't with the boxes. She needed to hunt it down.

Next, she went into the bathroom, looking around for something that she could easily sell for quick cash. There wasn't much, but she found his electric razor and she knew she could sell that easily enough at a pawn shop that didn't ask questions. The damn kid was obviously a trust-fund brat, so replacing his razor would be a short-lived inconvenience.

Passing back into his bedroom, she poked quickly through every drawer she could find looking for jewelry or cash stowed somewhere, but there was nothing. Growling under her breath, she decided this would have to be enough and to just get out of there before he came back up and caught her again. She took a quick look around the kitchen, even contemplated nicking the coffee machine, but decided it was too bulky to carry. She did find a plastic grocery bag and stowed the razor and the French press into it.

"I need to get out of here," she repeated to herself, feeling the old demon call to her. She was still moving too slow, and Elias could catch her at any moment. The old woman headed for the door, only to be deterred again by a glance at the bookshelves. Redirecting her route to the door, she peered through the shelves, considering for a moment if any of the books were valuable. Some of them certainly looked old enough, but she had no way to know for sure, and books were heavy. She did snatch up a shiny crystal decoration that looked like it could fetch something and a strange old watch that sat in a gap between the books. That's when she noticed that the left bookshelf had a handle in its side, just like the bookshelf on the right.

She stared at it for a long time.

"I should get out of here," she said out loud, echoing the angry voice inside her head, the one that had dominated most of her life and most of her decisions, especially after she met the demon on the street. It would not be pleased with her delay. "I should take what I have now and go."

But she didn't move. A lifetime of listening to that voice wasn't making her feet move any faster toward the door out.

"Maybe it's another staircase? Maybe it leads upstairs? There might be more things of value upstairs," she said to herself and timidly pulled on the handle. To her surprise, it moved easily. A light flickered on above her, revealing a staircase going up.

She wasn't sure what made her act so adventurous. Nothing in her life recently had motivated her like this. If she were to put a name to it, she would have to call it curiosity. So, up the stairs she went. As the secret door closed behind her, she almost felt like a truant, running away from school. She could imagine one of the nuns from her primary school days, stopping the door from closing at the last second to drag her back to class. They would have rapped her knuckles with a ruler for good measure. Even with that painful image, she grinned wickedly as she worked her way up, a step at a time.

Like below, a door waited above.

Blinking in surprise, Margaret stepped out into the large, cavernous room. It was dark with a ceiling that went up twice as high as the apartment below. Along the right wall was a row of shaded windows that let in the barest hint of light, along the other three walls, including the one where she came through, stood furniture covered in dusty white sheets. The floor was wood, and it seemed to be sprung, as if for dancing. There was nothing else of note.

"What would he need a ballroom for?" she asked the space out loud, her voice taking on a bit of an echo. She wasn't sure why she thought of it as a ballroom; a peeking under the sheets revealed no instruments or stage or anything. In disgust, she started to turn around to go back but stopped as she saw a pair of matching bookcases, like the floor below. If it was just like below, then the right one hid a door going downstairs and the left one...

After a moment's hesitation, she went over to the left one and pulled it open to reveal another staircase headed up.

The next secret door opened into another set of stairs that ended in a double-wide hallway, which made Margaret pause. Like everything in this building, the architecture was old, but also nice, like someone put some money into it. Though plain white, the halls were stuccoed in big swirling circles divided by rich, dark brown boards every few feet. Four doors set into the walls, two on each side and off-kilter to each other. She approached the first door slowly, half-expecting someone to jump out and demand to know what she was doing there. A brass plate was set squarely in the center. In perfect scroll, it read, *"Raymond Jacquet."* There were other plaques on the other three doors, but she couldn't read them. Not daring to go farther than that first door, Margaret knocked gently. Nothing. She knocked a little harder, the sound echoing faintly down the hallway. Nothing breathed or stirred. Gingerly, with much daring, Margaret gently pressed down on the curlicue door handle.

That feeling washed over her again as she passed over the threshold, the one of wrongness that she never could place. Inside, the room was the shadowy dark of drawn shades against the bright light of mid-day. A man sat in a chair. Or at least...

Margaret blinked and looked again.

There was no one else in the room.

"Hello?" she called out, just in case. She could have sworn she saw someone.

"Just a ghost," she answered herself. She had seen them before. Another reason to not stay sober. It made the visions of the long-dead not bother her as much. "Nothing to see here but the snoopy old lady," she offered as an explanation to whatever apparition lingered.

When nothing moved in reaction to her intrusion, Margaret grew bolder and flipped on the light switch. Instead of the glare of an overhead light, a single lamp came to life next to the comfiest looking La-Z-Boy recliner Margaret had ever seen. Overstuffed bookshelves framed the tableau. Mostly paperbacks in neat rows, their perfect uniformity interrupted every so often by the lone hardcover. A fine layer of dust coated everything.

Margaret didn't read very well. So often she'd been told she was too stupid. Over time, she had let that lie become truth. Still, the place looked like a library to her. In the still fairly shadowy room, she realized bookshelves lined most of the walls, equally stuffed with books and magazines. On the wall opposite the chair, a card table interrupted the line of shelves. Hung above the table was a map of the world. Pushpins of different colors connected with equally colored string crisscrossed the map with most of the concentrations between Central Europe and Africa. On the card table, several books laid nicely arranged as if someone had cleaned them up, but didn't bother to shelve them. The topmost tome simply stated "World War II" in gold embossed seraph characters on the thickly textured, fawn-colored cover.

Turning away, Margaret spied a bit of kitchen in the corner. The mid-ranged appliances waited quietly, looking as clean as a showroom, except dust enough to write a memoir in covered everything.

Finding nothing in the kitchen she could easily take and hock, like silverware or something, Margaret moved to the bedroom, picking up her feet so as not to make any noise. The longer she spent in the room, the more she felt like she was in a church or a graveyard. An expectant, holy solemnity fell over her like a shawl. Which was why the loud squeak of the bedroom door as it opened inward made her flinch.

In the way the living room was covered in books, the bedroom walls were covered in pictures. Most were in color, but a few were in black and white. Margaret gravitated to those first. They were closest to the bed, which was pushed into the corner. Each image hung in a silver frame arranged in a sort of chaotic pattern. Leaning in, she looked at the images of a young, handsome man, his skin a rich darkness that stood out strongly in the grey world he inhabited. He was dressed in a military uniform, but not one she recognized. Possibly World War II era, but the insignias on his chest and lapel were unfamiliar as was the emblem on the front of his rounded helmet. He stared very seriously into the camera, which somehow had managed to capture the twinkle of purpose in his eyes.

Two other photos of the same man hung next to the first. The next picture captured an image of two soldiers, one of which was the purposeful young man. Both men were chest-high in a trench that had to be covered in snow because it was almost too white as it framed them. Between the men stood a Gatling gun, manned by the first soldier as his companion fed the string of bullets into it. They were both looking at the photographer when the image was snapped. The purposeful man's eyes were a little more haunted, but no more lacking in purpose.

The third picture was of the same soldier, but he stood in a group. A few other uniformed men stood among them, two of them Tigermen. They were amongst others, standing in civilian clothes that reminded Margaret of the iconography of the French Resistance. Most were human, though a large fellow in a flat, newsboy cap was definitely a troll. Antlers stuck out from the top of the crowd, but the face of the possible faun was obscured by a woman with short, wavy hair. All of their faces were pale and weary. They were all focusing on something off to the soldiers' right outside of the photo. Young people with serious faces, reflecting how wrong those times really were.

Fascinated, Margaret moved on to the next images to her right. These were in bright color with the sharp detail of modern, enhanced prints. Several featured an old man, his skin dulled and framed with grey, but those eyes... They were the same as the young soldier's. Many of the pictures were in front of monuments and flags, the old man the center focus of each.

She was particularly taken with a shot of the old man looking off into a sunset, a sweet peace on his tired face. Her fingers reached up to touch the frame gently, which made it spark and change color. Margaret gasped as the image in the frame wavered and disappeared, only to be replaced with a new image. The same old man, this time with Elias standing next to him, his arm over the decidedly shorter man's shoulders, his other arm stretching toward the edge of the image, like he was one-handedly taking a picture. Blinking twice, Margaret gingerly tapped the edge of the frame again. Like before, it wavered, and another image materialized, this one of the old man standing inside an old-looking building amongst a small crowd of dignified-looking people. They were all gazing at something the picture didn't show, until the next tap. That image was a wider one of the previous and included a coffin covered in a French flag as well as the corner of a second one caught on the edge of the frame.

"The Memoriam for the French Resistance fighters," a voice explained.

Margaret spun around to find Elias standing in the bedroom doorway. It was obvious that he had been watching her for a while. He continued talking, ignoring her startled expression. "Took me three months to persuade him to go. He hadn't been invited, though by all rights he should have been. I heard about it in some culture column, I don't even remember which paper now. He was so sure they wouldn't let us in."

He stopped speaking, having crossed into the room to stand next to her, his gaze never leaving the picture or the past. "I made him bring his commission papers. Raymond was a soldier in the Franco-African forces when I met him the first time..." Elias traced a finger up to another frame and tapped it, making it flash colors as he talked until he found the image he wanted.

It was of himself, looking the same age, young and handsome, but with short, shaggy hair stuffed under a newsboy cap, as if there hadn't been time to cut it properly. He wore a dark, buttoned coat and a ruffled, rough-looking, dull-white shirt. This image was strange, warped around the edges and weirdly colored.

"This can't be you," Margaret said, peering hard at Elias's image.

"Why not?"

She shook her head.

"Or at least...I mean...it's a re-enactment thing, right?"

Elias shook his head. "Not at all."

"It's in color!" She jabbed a finger at his vibrant blue eyes in the image.

He sighed. "Yes, it is."

"Then it can't be authentic!" she roared, driving her point as hard as she could. Why was he working so hard to trick her like this?

"As you wish," he acquiesced, tapping the frame back to its original picture.

Though she had won her argument, Margaret didn't feel at all like she had. Why was she arguing about it anyway? Something about this whole story he told her felt so wrong, like a vision she didn't want to see. What did this damn kid think he was trying to pull? She wasn't stupid.

"When France honored the four resistance fighters..." He pulled another frame off the wall. It was a newspaper clipping, with the headline that read: FRENCH RESISTANCE HEROES INDUCTED INTO THE PANTHEON IN PARIS. Elias's eyes wandered over the clipping, looking deeper than the thin ink on the tender paper could possibly be. He licked his lips and water glinted at the corner of his eyes. "We *had* to go."

Margaret didn't know what to say. He replaced the clipping back on the wall, then slid his hands into his pockets and stepped away, tossing his shoulders up into a sigh.

"Well, anyway. This is Raymond's room."

"Where is he?" Margaret asked, her stomach clenching. Nothing in the room looked like it had been disturbed in a long time.

"He died three years ago."

She took a step back. "How?"

"Cancer. The systemic kind that no amount of medicine or magic could fix. Not without killing him faster. We were only together for six years."

"Together, how?"

"Like I would like to be with you." He responded to her question, but despite the simplicity of his answer, something still felt off about it. Nothing about him seemed as it had the day before, but Margaret struggled to put her finger on the difference. He was still beautiful and young, but maybe not as young as she had first thought. No, at that moment, he seemed like, well, a full-fledged adult. There was a set to his expression, the kind that young men rarely achieved until past their twenties into their thirties when they finally went from raw boys to finished men.

The shift disturbed Margaret, but it was unsurprising. She had seen it before. Men never showed their true nature, not until it was too late. Now, as she looked at him, those same eyes that had smiled so gleefully the day before were dark blue and sad, and very, very wrong.

Blinking again, Margaret thought, for the briefest of moments, she saw the other man, Raymond, standing over Elias's shoulder. He also looked at the photos. One moment the ghost seemed young, the next, old. Then Raymond turned to her, meeting her gaze. In the span of her blink, the ghost was gone. She blinked a few more times and focused on Elias. Silver light resonated off of him, highlighting his features. Margaret's breath caught as she realized what was happening. She had seen this light before, but she didn't know what it was or what it meant. Only that it occurred around certain people and was always connected to the ghosts.

Unheeding of her growing panic, Elias adjusted the pictures on the wall again, giving Margaret an opening to glance back at the door. How fast could she run at this point? Not fast enough, even with her patched up hip.

"Where are you going?" Elias asked.

He didn't look directly at her, but rather at the bag in her arms with her small collection of loot.

She backpedaled, then jutted out her chin. "I'm leaving."

He sniffed. "I see."

That was all he was going to say? He knew she was robbing him, and that was it? Feeling the weight of the objects, she let them drop. "Fuck you," she growled and turned to run away from the sick feeling in her stomach.

"Would you like some cash? It would be easier to carry."

"Go to hell," she shot back and kept walking. She didn't need this shit. She didn't need to be judged. Seething with those thoughts, she made her way down the stairs, through his apartment, and back to the building's front door, the one that led to the outside world, barely knowing how she got there. She clawed at the knob, but it failed to open. While she screeched at the inanimate object, his hand appeared and turned the knob.

Another thrum of wrongness washed over her as Elias pulled the door open to get it out of her way. Still raging, she grabbed the outer handle, pulling control of the door from Elias to slam it shut behind her.

Cold slapped her hard in the face the minute Margaret got her feet on the street. The sweater she wore was woefully inadequate, but going back for the coat would mean…going back. Wrapping her arms around herself, the old woman decided she could tough it out long enough to find someplace else to be. Any place else.

Except, as she stared at the day street, with its few people and plenty of cars moving by on the cold, clean autumnal day, she had no idea where to go next. That usually wasn't a problem; wandering the streets looking for the answer to the next creature comfort had been plenty for her. But now she wasn't hungry, didn't need the bathroom, didn't need a shower, and she didn't want company. She didn't need anything, except maybe a coat. With that as a guiding purpose, Margaret turned and walked to the end of the block, looking for street signs to help her get her bearings.

She was actually surprised that her unwanted host hadn't followed her out onto the street, or even done more to stop her. A stealthy glance back verified that his door was closed and he wasn't anywhere to be seen. The least the idiot could have done was chase after her with the coat.

What did she care, anyway? Her death wasn't back there.

The signs at the end of the block were unfamiliar, giving her no clue as to where she was in the city, so she kept trudging. After three blocks, the wind had cut through any warmth the sweater had carried with her from the apartment. She began to shiver. Finally, she turned off into an alley to get out of the wind. The winter cold from Lake Superior seemed to always come long before the snow. It took her breath away.

What was she doing? Sure, she wanted to die, but if it were by freezing to death, she could have done that decades ago. Only idiots died by freezing.

She just about talked herself into turning around and going back for that coat, begging for it if she had to, when two men stalked out of the dark.

"You lost, grandma?"

Normally, hooligans like these ignored her, and she ignored them. There was no point in harassing someone like her unless they knew for certain she had something they wanted. Usually, her worn, dirty clothing and her smell kept most of them away. Yet, here she was, dressed in clean, new clothes with no telltale smell of poverty and desperation to ward them off. She actually did look like someone's grandma.

"Hey, Hey, grandma. I'm talking to you." One of the men got closer, his warm, tanned skin lightening as he leaned into the sunlight to try to force her to meet his eyes. Margaret tucked her head to the side, stubbornly refusing to look at him. "Hey!" he shouted.

"Hey! Don't yell at her, man; you're going to scare her," his companion said as he cornered her, placing himself between her and the street.

The first man attempted to grip her chin to force her to look up.

Automatically, Margaret slapped his hand away. "Don't touch me."

The man chuckled. "Boy, you are feisty, aren't you?" He yielded a little space as he straightened up. "Where are you supposed to be, ma'am?"

"None of your business."

"Okay, fine." The man crossed his arms. "How about telling me what day it is today?"

Margaret wasn't sure what game this was, but she ground what remained of her teeth and glanced up. "Tuesday, or..." she paused at that, realizing that wasn't right. "...Wednesday."

"Uh-huh. How about who's the president?"

She double blinked. "What the hell does that matter?"

"Can you tell me your name, grandma?" he asked instead of answering.

"Hey Joey, do you think I should just call 911?" his companion asked, pulling out a scratched-up old flip phone from his neon-colored windbreaker.

"Yeah, we might have to. If we can't find where she belongs, they can at least get her somewhere warm."

The bottom dropped out of Margaret's stomach. It was bad enough they thought she was someone's moneyed grandma; they obviously also thought she had Alzheimer's. The thought of being institutionalized again terrified her more than being cold on the street.

"Leave me alone," she snapped and tried to push past the two men, back toward the street. Naturally, she didn't succeed.

"Now, stay here a second, grandma," the man named Joey said, blocking her. "We're not going to hurt you, but you got no business being out here without a coat."

"Why don't we take her over to the coffee shop at the end there? Have them call somebody?"

"Yeah, maybe you're right." Joey shrugged.

"I ain't going anywhere with you," she snapped and pushed back even more violently.

"Hey!" Joey shouted, actually knocked back in surprise at her strength. She only gained ground because he wasn't expecting it. Before he could recover, she turned to head further into the alley.

She was so distracted by the two men calling and grabbing after her that she didn't see the encroaching darkness until it was too late. Despite it being a sunny day, the deeper part of the alley remained unnaturally dim, like a heavy storm was approaching. The walls were blackened like someone had burned them. When Margaret stopped to look closer, she could see the darkness slowly crawling across the brick. Out of that darkness, a tiny baby cried.

The men didn't seem to see or hear anything unusual; they remained focused on pulling her back toward the street, like animals sensing danger that they couldn't actually see.

Margaret knew she could walk into that darkness. She knew if she wanted, the darkness would intercede for her, bring her closer to itself and deal with these men who interfered with her. It had done so before. To prove its point, it made the men let go of her arms. Absentmindedly, they both started walking out onto the bright street, as they had intended to do if they hadn't encountered her.

"Wait..." she breathed softly. She didn't want to go back into the darkness. She never did; it was just the only choice she had ever had. The darkness recoiled from her as if it heard her thoughts and was surprised.

"*Wait?*"

The two men stopped at the end of the alley, turning to talk to someone briefly before the one called Joey pointed toward her. Then the darkness possessing them, making them glassy-eyed and helpless, faded. They looked confused as they continued to speak to whoever stood just out of sight. A hand appeared and shook the two men's in turn. At each touch, clean light seemed to cleanse what the darkness had corrupted. Both men smiled and waved as they headed away down the street.

As they retreated, Elias stepped forward to fill the space they had left. He carried her coat. The one he had bought for her.

For a moment, Margaret felt the darkness harden, like it wanted to claw into her, but for some reason it couldn't.

You don't want him to see you, the darkness purred as it tried to obscure her vision, increasing itself around her, but all it seemed to do was make Elias shine brighter. And he did shine. A gold-white corona surrounded his body, highlighting his features in beautiful relief that sculptors sold their souls to achieve.

"What is he?" Margaret whispered out loud, staring at him through the darkness. It felt like she suddenly saw so much more of him, like she had up in Raymond's room. He was something more than a man, more than any man she had ever seen.

Who cares? He can't save you, the demon in the darkness responded as the beautiful, young man approached her. *You're not worthy of being saved, even if he could. Nobody would want you anyway.*

"Nobody would want me anyway," she repeated, barely louder than a breath.

"Okay, I give up," Elias said as he held out the coat for her to put on. "I thought I could just let you walk away, but I'm an idiot." She stared at the coat. "Here," he insisted, as he took each shoulder to hold for her.

Compliantly, she turned and let him slip the coat up her arms and over her shoulders. "You don't have to come home with me, but could we walk for a ways?"

"You can take me to a coffee shop," she said. When the two men mentioned coffee before, it had actually sounded pretty good.

She felt the darkness coil behind her, watching menacingly. Elias didn't seem to see it. Maybe that only meant Margaret *was* crazy. Totally cracked to think that there was actually a darkness with a demon in it that followed her around and talked to her. The black demon had to be a metaphor for her drug use. She had taken drugs for so long…yes, her going off her nut made more sense. It simply did, and she much preferred simple explanations at that moment.

She *had* to be crazy. She walked away from a beautiful, wonderful man like Elias.

He smiled at her, and she quivered inside. "Yeah, great. I know a really nice not-too-corporate place where we can go." He connected the ends of her zipper and drew the toggle up just under her chin. She let him, encasing her in a feeling of warmth that was already taking the place of the cold. Then he offered her his arm to lead her away from the alley.

The darkness stalked at a distance, but Margaret ignored it.

CHAPTER 5

"I WANT TO APOLOGIZE TO YOU," ELIAS SAID AFTER THEY HAD STROLLED a few blocks.

"What for?" Margaret asked.

"Specifically...for not having any sort of plan." He stared off as they waited for the traffic light to change. Margaret simply enjoyed being, walking out in the open, in the sunshine, amongst people. For the first time, she felt like looking about herself; the world had truly changed to her. A tune started playing in her head. The walk sign flashed, and, as he led her across the street, she started to hum it softly to herself. After a few bars, the words emerged and, almost unbidden, replaced her humming.

"...no, I never heard them at all, 'til there was you." She blinked in surprise, for the first time understanding that pretty song.

"What was that?" Elias asked.

Margaret blushed and, for a moment, almost told him to mind his own business but, instead, she stopped herself and reconsidered. "Just a song I heard a long time ago. I was just thinking how now I...I think I get what it was talking about."

"Music Man, right?" he supplied. "I had to play the chorus in my head to remember it."

"Yeah," she said softly.

He chuckled softly. "I knew you knew the songs."

The conversation died there.

They walked together quietly until they stopped for a string of pre-school children, bookended by their teachers, slowly making their way toward the park. Margaret felt her chest constrict at the sight of the little ones, toddling very seriously by, in their little coats, hats, and gloves.

"Why didn't you take the coat?" Elias asked, a heartbeat before she pulled away to retreat. She thought for a moment that he meant more than what he asked, but as she regarded him, his question seemed to be genuine, oblivious to her internal reaction to the sight of the children.

"I didn't need..." No. That was a lie. She hadn't thought when she stormed out. Otherwise, she would have grabbed the coat. And once she was on the street, she'd been too full of pride to go back for it.

"Margaret, how long have you sought your death?"

The children had finally passed with an acknowledging nod from their trailing caretaker. They began walking again.

"You would think it wouldn't be so hard to find. So many others die so easy," she answered. "Why did you save *me*?"

He *hmmph*ed. "You looked so worn and weary and hard. I kept thinking as I watched you dig through the trash...that it wasn't fair."

"What wasn't?"

"You didn't deserve to end like that."

"You don't know that."

"I mean, maybe, but in my experience, very few people deserve suffering and, even then, not forever. You looked..." his eyes were far away as he spoke, "you looked like you had suffered enough. I wanted to give you peace. I wanted to give you a good end to your life. I thought, to die in the arms of someone who...cares for you, that would be justice." He blinked as he came back to the here and now. He turned a small gentle smile to her. "Except you didn't die."

"I never do. Sorry to disappoint," she replied.

He barked a laugh. "That's just fine. Serves me right for deciding your fate for you." He slowed and stretched out a hand to pull a wooden door filled with glass open for her. "Here we are."

Margaret looked up at the storefront. "A bar?"

"Eh, I decided I wanted lunch more than coffee. Come on, this place is wonderful."

The inside of the bar was warmly lit and full of laughter. Somewhere, Margaret heard shouts and loud music, but in the room they entered, the atmosphere was much more subdued and chattier. There was a long bar along the right wall, with plenty of people around it giving and receiving drink orders. Tables were spread out in the space, most filled with more people talking and enjoying plates of food with drinks. Overall, it seemed like an average pub except for the many-colored, twinkling lights darting through the air. And the devil sitting in the only booth in the room.

At the sight of the devil, Margaret froze in the doorway, staring at him. It took her a moment to realize the devil wasn't real, but a statue painted to look like one. The statue sat, dressed in a suit with a jaunty hat perched on top of its head, one small horn poking through the brim and another curling around the lip of the hat. His face was frozen mid-laugh, with one arm draped over the back of the booth, and the other gripping an empty low-ball glass.

"It's okay, walk on in," Elias said from behind her as he let the door fall closed. Margaret had no choice but to go the rest of the way inside.

"Elias is here!" a tiny, musical voice cried. Many of the floating lights squealed and rushed over to the young man, swirling their colors around his head like a rainbow halo. Elias laughed and gently batted the small faeries away.

He glanced over at her mischievously, which faltered into a raised eyebrow.

"What?" Margaret asked, a little defensively.

"I'm not sure. You don't seem amazed."

"Oh," she looked around again. "I mean, it's a nice bar..."

"The faeries," he said, cutting her off as he gestured at the dancing crowd around his head.

"What about them? They're faeries."

"It's just..." now his cheeks flushed an embarrassed red, "Well, most hominals, humans, from outside the magical community, they can get kind of..."

Margaret crossed her arms as she waited for him to finish, but his words drained away, so she finally threw him a bone. "I've seen faeries before. There are faeries everywhere in this city. Especially on the streets."

"Come in already, you're causing a ruckus," a gruff voice ordered, and the little faeries scattered in a chorus of laughter.

"Hello, Alf. Thought I would come in for lunch," Elias greeted. At first, Margaret couldn't see who he was talking to until the bartender stepped up, popping up from behind the bar. He was obviously a little person, and everything about him seemed tough.

The bartender leaned on one elbow as he cocked his opposing fist against his hip. "It's a bit rushed right now."

"Is the Lady of the House in?" Elias asked, surveying the tables.

"No, she isn't," Alf said curtly. "She's out."

Elias's eyes narrowed, his brows puckering together. "Out where?"

"Devil if I know. She's with that corporate pretty-boy again."

Elias huffed a little, then turned to Margaret and put an arm around her shoulders, pulling her closer. "Alf, this is Margaret, Margaret, this is Alf."

The little man nodded at her. "Ma'am." The roughness disappeared a moment as he took Margaret in. "Can I get you something to drink?"

"Uh, a coffee…" Margaret started softly, suddenly feeling shy. That was stupid. Who comes to a bar to get a coffee?

"Coffee straight or boozy?" Elf, or Alf, she wasn't too sure which it was, said without batting an eye. "I have a very nice hot boozy coffee cocktail I can put together. Brandy, Marnier, Kahlua, coffee, twist of orange."

Margaret couldn't suppress her smile. "That sounds… amazing."

"Yeah, it really does. I'll have one too." Elias took Margaret's hand. "Come on, I see a table open."

Elias led her by the hand to the table in question. He pulled out her chair for her and sat her down.

Margaret cast an eye over the place again. "So, you all do very well for yourselves, don't you?" she said more than asked.

"You'd think that." He shrugged. He had plucked up a small menu to look at but didn't seem to be actually reading it. "But that's not what we're here to talk about right now, anyway."

They both lapsed into a heavy, acute silence. It was uncomfortable. Margaret fidgeted, turning an eye toward the Devil sitting a few feet away, his back to their table.

"It's a tourist gimmick," Elias said, pulling her attention back, giving her a smile that was both happy and sad.

"It's fine," Margaret said, proceeding to stare at their own table. More silence.

"Margaret," Elias said, shifting so he leaned on his crossed arms, looking away to see if the words he wanted were on the floor.

She beat him to it; the table was more forthcoming. "Why did you take *me* in? Why me out of every other homeless old lady?"

"Honestly…" he stopped and then deflated, "it was on a whim."

"Obviously," Margaret said dryly.

"You looked like you were barely there. Strung out and fragile, like Raymond did before he went. Taking care of him in his final days…were the…" His voice became thick with emotion. He swallowed down to continue. "It gave me purpose, and I got a lot of things from knowing him and caring for him that I'm even now trying to sort out. In that time, I was my best self. Or at least a better self than I had been in years."

"And you tried to capture that again with me?" She picked at the corner of the abandoned menu on the table. Well, as long as they were confessing things… "I always thought my death would be painful and cruel. A punishment. You saw it as peace. Neither of us got what we expected since I didn't have the good sense to give up the ghost."

"What I wanted was wrong. I'm sorry, Margaret." Then he paused and shifted. "And you don't deserve to be murdered."

She snorted, and he furrowed his brow.

"Is that what you believe?" he asked.

"You don't have a clue about what I deserve. You've barely started your life, or barely done anything so horrible to be even close to understanding or conceiving of what I have done. Trust me, kid, I deserve my suffering."

He stared at her, but she wouldn't look at him. His silence said plenty. She felt his anger building.

"I am over two hundred and fifty years old," he stated.

Margaret blinked rapidly. "What?"

"I'd have to do some math to figure out my exact age. After the first hundred, hundred and fifty years, you stop keeping real track."

"That's... that's impossible..." she said, as a small faerie alighted on their table.

"Are you ready to order?" the small person asked. Her tiny, near translucent wings flickered rhythmically as she adjusted the equally tiny devil horns tied to her fuzzy green hair.

"Tippy, would you give us a few more minutes?" Elias asked.

"Yeah, sure," the faerie said, not at all reading the emotions at the table as she rose up a little into the air. "Should I put in loaded potato skins for you?"

"Sounds perfect, thank you," Elias said. The little fae made a loop-de-loop in the air before disappearing into the kitchen.

"You're lying," Margaret said the second he turned his attention back to her.

"I often do. Not in this moment, however," he said like he didn't truly care what she thought about his statement.

"You said you weren't a vampire." Margaret racked her brain for some scrap of knowledge she had that she could understand and cling to.

"Vampire's don't live for very long, contrary to popular cultural perceptions. Those natural-born live the same lifespan as humans. Magic-based ones die quicker than if they had stayed mortal, in most cases. I am neither of those."

"But what about...what about..." Margaret drew a blank. There were many kinds of peoples in the world, and she had ignored all of them most of her life. She simply could not care less about their troubles. She had enough of her own. "Then... what are you?"

"I'm me," he stated.

She had to suppress the urge to slug him.

Margaret looked around the room at the various devil kitsch and the faeries dancing in the air. Several of the other customers were non-hominal. A dancing garbage can rushed back and forth behind the stools of the bar collecting peanut shells. She thought back to the things she had seen in Elias's shop.

"So, you're actually a wizard?" she concluded.

"Professionally? Technically, yes, but that's not..." he sighed. "Look, what I am is irrelevant, isn't it? Don't ask me to explain it."

"Why?"

He snorted a huff. "That's an example of asking."

She crossed her arms stubbornly. While they stared each other down, Alf came up to the table personally with the drinks and potato skins on a tray. Setting it all down between them on the table, he took both of them in.

"You're dating him, aren't you?" Alf asked Margaret, jabbing a thumb at Elias. "You've got that look."

"No, I am not," Margaret said.

"Uh-huh, sure. Well, please taste the drink first before you throw it in his face." With that, Alf turned and went back toward his bar.

"Alf, wait a second," Elias called.

"What?" the bar manager groused.

"How old am I?"

"Hell, if I know," Alf snapped, throwing his hands up into the air. "Two hundred something, right?" Then he tromped off.

"Thanks, Alf," Elias called after him but kept his grinning eyes on Margaret.

She pursed her lips. "Well, then, if you *are* two hundred and fifty years old, and you're not a vampire or something, why do you look the way you do?"

"It's just natural to who I am."

"That's lucky," she sniffed.

"Yes, but to get back to my earlier point, I've been around a lot longer than you, *kid*." He paused, pointedly laying the term on her in exactly the same manner she had laid it on him. "Whatever you have done in your life, whatever mistakes you've made, you do not deserve to suffer for it the rest of your life. I've lived four times as many lifetimes as you have and I can assure you, I have done much more than you could possibly imagine." He took a deep drink from his glass, his Adam's apple bobbing with each swallow.

"I said taste the drink!" Alf could be heard shouting from his bar, but neither one of them responded to it.

Elias set his glass back on the table. "And as to the other question you keep implying, about why haven't I chosen to pursue a younger woman...why on earth would I want to be with someone who has barely lived? Kids are all questions, seeking answers that even, after all these years, I just don't always have. I would rather talk to someone like you who already understands a piece of this thing we call life."

Margaret didn't know what to say to any of that. It was all too much. What *could* she say? Instead, she reached out for something that at least made sense and wrapped her fingers around her coffee cup.

It was barely warm anymore, and the whipped cream on top made it seem more like a dessert than a drink, but it was still coffee. Carefully, she brought the mug up to her lips and sipped. A sharp pain sparked in her mouth.

Squeaking, she set the cup down hard on the table, her hands flying up to her jaw, where the pain still sparked.

"Margaret? Are you okay?" Elias asked, but she was already moving.

Before she realized it, she had landed in the restroom, the light coming on automatically. She stopped in front of the sinks, the pain getting worse. With one finger, she felt inside her mouth. With just a light touch, knife-sharp pain stung through her gums as something came loose. Falling out of her mouth, it clinked on the porcelain of the sink. A streak of red appeared, slashing across the bowl, ending in a brown lump.

Leaving her one hand to cover her mouth, her other fingers picked up the rotted remains of an old tooth. She had seen this before, so it wasn't so shocking that she had lost yet another one. Usually, she just threw them away and continued on with whatever she was doing. Setting it on the edge of the sink, she dared to look up at the mirror. Despite her hatred of her reflection, she was seized with a desire to see which tooth had fallen out.

She stared at her blinking self. The same damn old lady stared back at her, but she seemed different from a few days ago when Elias had made her see herself as she was. Pushing aside any desire for further emotional self-examination, she opened her mouth, hardly shocked to see exactly what she expected to see; a handful of browned, rotted teeth, poking out of bright red gums. Gently, she probed at the spot where blood still welled out a bit. It didn't sting anymore, which was something. She brushed away the blood, looking for the gaping hole that should have been left behind.

Except it wasn't there. Instead, there was a small, bright white spot. She rubbed her eyes rapidly and looked again, pulling away a bit at her reddened gum. It was there. Truly there. A new, white tooth poked through in the spot where her lower left canine used to be. The old woman's face—Margaret's face in the mirror was flabbergasted.

She closed her mouth, then opened it again.

It was still there.

What did this mean? The old, dead, brown tooth was still in her hand and a white new tooth in her mouth. A *white* tooth.

What was happening to her?

She was *changing.*

Then, she could feel it. The darkness still beckoning to her outside of this place. It couldn't come close to her when she was with Elias.

Margaret, you don't deserve redemption, the darkness crowed, its voice distant, yet still clear.

"He says I do."

He's lying. You know he's lying. Why would he want someone like you?

"Why would he want someone like me?" she repeated. Why *would* someone like him want someone like her unless he was...And then Margaret could see it; exactly what Elias was hiding, what the demon in the darkness didn't want her to realize, what it feared about Elias.

Elias was an angel. Maybe one forced into mortal existence, pretending to be a wizard, and working magic to disguise his miracles, which would make her someone he had chosen to save!

With acute urgency, Margaret left the restroom, clutching her dead tooth in her hand, her proof that her theory was correct. He waited for her outside, eyebrows pinched in worry, his arms crossed. She stopped at the sight of him, so young-looking and handsome, but there was something ancient and wise in his eyes.

"Is everything alright?" he asked.

Of course, he would ask. He was kind like that. Margaret's chest warmed at his concern, as she fingered the tooth in her hand, torn about whether to show him or not.

You do not deserve to be happy.

"Did you mean it?" she asked.

Elias raised a questioning eyebrow. Dammit, he was going to make her ask, or beg actually. It was a simple thing to do. She realized, like a long-locked door finally bring pried open, that everything she ever wanted stood right in front of her; she simply had to ask for it. Ask for forgiveness. Except the problem with asking was he could answer no. Everyone else had. And he would be right to. He was a good being, and she was unworthy. Yet, the thought of returning to the street and the darkness made her feel sick. For the first time in too long, she felt the grief that drugs and alcohol and magic had suppressed for her. Like a disease, the sickness spread through her. Inevitably, the burning coal of her pride ignited with anger, that false shield she used against the world began to flare, giving her chin stubbornness, silencing wisdom that cried, pleaded, don't do this. Don't walk away from him again.

"Please come home with me," Elias asked. He ran his hand through his hair and tugged on his ear.

Margaret blinked.

Elias opened his hand and held it out to her. "Please, stay with me and live out the rest of your days with me. I promise to make them as happy as I possibly can."

She stared at his hand, her mind processing that he was actually saying what she wanted so badly to hear. "You want me to stay with you? Forever?"

"Yes. Please, please stay with me. I will take care of you splendidly. Your last years will be peaceful and safe, I promise."

The old woman waved her hand dismissively. "And then when you're done with me, you'll kill me?"

He sighed and shook his head. "I mean, I will stay with you until the day you die, since I think we can both agree that I will outlive you."

"That goes without saying," she agreed. Laughter came from the bar. Margaret checked, but no one was coming. It was like they were in their own little bubble of space, floating outside the busyness of the world beyond. "Well, you can't want me for my money, I don't have any."

"Everything that I have I will share with you."

That made Margaret blink. "You want to get married?"

A look of doubt crossed Elias's face. Margaret took some satisfaction in finally ruffling that pristine serenity.

"Ah," she said with smug judgment. "I see how it is."

"I just...don't do long-term commitments," he hedged awkwardly.

Margaret wasn't going to let him off the hook. "Which is why you go looking for the living corpses?"

"Do you need something formal like that?" he asked.

That made her pause. The small voice inside said yes, but that was a ridiculous notion, getting married at her age. "No. No, I don't." His hand was still outstretched to her, waiting. She placed her own gently in his, accepting his warmth and his strength and his proposal. "Since you asked so nicely."

"That's fine." He laced his fingers in between hers; strong, smooth fingers, framed her wrinkled, smaller ones.

"And if anything happens that I don't like, I'm gone," she added, a sense of inner peace flooding her.

He squeezed gently.

Somewhere far away, the darkness growled.

CHAPTER 6

Margaret's newfound inner peace didn't last through the night.

"What the hell is this?"

"Are you going to be shocked every time I feed you?" Elias asked, sliding the spoon next to the bowl. In the middle of the island counter was a tray with several canisters filled with toppings for oatmeal. "Dress it up how you like. I have to be down in the store today, so you are on your own."

"What am I? An orphan or a kept woman?" she muttered, staring down the bowl of oatmeal like it offended her.

"Got a headache?" he asked as he picked up a black belt that was sitting on the counter to lace it through the loops of his dress slacks. He had to lift up his black button-down shirt to do it. Margaret couldn't help watching the whole process under her hooded lids. For a man as old as he claimed to be, the space of hard belly peeking out from under that shirt was tempting. To cover up her perusal, she drank down the waiting cup of coffee while it was still too hot. He had woken something inside her the other day, not that she had any intention of admitting that.

"You're dressing up?"

"Yes."

She huffed. He was playing his obtuse game again. "Why?"

"Because I look good like this, don't I?" He held out his arms and turned on the spot so she could see him from every angle. Of course, the man didn't have a single bad one.

"Looks fine," she pretended to dismiss him as she sat on the stool.

After he had tucked her into his bed the night before, she had fallen asleep hard, though she had no memory of it until she awoke the next morning. Maybe she was going to sleep the rest of her life away. Leaning her forehead on one hand, she massaged her right temple, trying to let up the pressure behind her right eye.

"You should drink more water. I also have some Acetaminophen if you want," her new friend offered, as he finished tucking his shirt into his pants.

"You have what?" she groused.

"Tylenol," he said and opened a cupboard above the sink to pull out a large, standard-white, plastic bottle. He placed it next to her coffee cup before pouring a clear glass of water as well.

She stared at it as if he had poured her liquid acid. She didn't like this. His behavior was definitely different that morning. All business-like and detached. Previous mornings, he had been mooning like a lovesick calf.

"What do your neighbors think about your lifestyle, buggering old ladies?"

He didn't smile this time. "Not much, since we don't really have neighbors. I more or less own the whole building. We're the only ones here," he said matter-of-factly.

Margaret almost dropped her coffee. "The whole building!"

"Yes. Two other floors going up, and the one below. The whole building. I own this whole building." Elias walked over to the twin set of bookshelves as he fixed his shirt back into place. Again, like magic, he pulled open the right bookcase, and the light above flickered on. "It's more or less financially tied up in such a way that I can't really sell it, so I might as well live here. I bought it after the war."

"Which war?"

Elias smiled. "If you get bored up here, you can always come downstairs," he said, stepping down a couple of steps toward his store.

"You expect me to go down more stairs?"

"You can also take the elevator, it goes to every floor. I bet you take the stairs though," he said.

"Why is that?"

"You strike me as a very stubborn lady." He flashed her his smile and disappeared down the stairs, his fancy square-toed shoes making arrhythmic clacking sounds as he practically leaped down them.

"Stupid mother fucker," Margaret muttered, then coughed a dry chuckle. "Grandmother fucker." Not that she was. And not that they had. As far as she knew.

Staring down at the oatmeal for a few minutes, she drank her straight black coffee. The old suspicions she had lived her life by came slipping back in. There was no way she was going to touch the mushy oats. Who knew what he put in it? Oatmeal was that bland sort of food that people over-filled with other flavors so you couldn't taste what else was inside. In past cases, it would be medicine or something. Not that she could reasonably think he had done that. But, if he had, he needed to tell her first, not trick her like all those nurses did the last time she'd been put away.

Sighing, she got up and poured herself some more coffee from his fancy-schmancy French press. There was no way she was going to turn down the coffee. He could put whatever the hell he wanted to into that and she'd drink it anyway. She pushed down the little voice in her head that said *that* was contrary thinking. The little voice had gotten a lot bolder lately.

Sipping the fresh drink, she rolled the taste around on her tongue and unbidden a memory bubbled up. She was back in her mother's kitchen of that crappy apartment with the hole in the wall. It had always smelled like a bathroom. Her mother was busy; she was always busy whenever Margaret was concerned, and Margaret was hungry. The radio was playing some new song, except it was an old, old song now, the words just outside the edge of little Margaret's vocabulary. She was picking at crumbs on the floor when she saw her mother's abandoned chipped cup. The first sip had been disgusting, but it had also warmed Margaret's insides; she drank down the whole thing before her mother came back. She had thought her mother would be angry, but instead, seeing her with the empty cup in both hands had made her mother laugh, truly and deeply, braying out full-throated guffaws so hard she rocked in place for breath. Margaret had loved coffee ever since.

She had worked in a coffee shop once for a while, serving coffee to rough, self-important, working men, who would pinch her bottom and tell her to smile because it pleased them to make her feel small and powerless. Dumping coffee onto the last one's lap had been worth it. She grinned at the memory. Coffee had been her weapon of choice, and she had no regrets.

Old Margaret set the newly empty cup back on the counter.

So, what was she supposed to do now? She usually filled her days looking for food, begging for change, or finding a warm place to sit her aching body, but all those needs were met, so what was left to her?

Sitting there in the empty apartment, Margaret could see her whole life laid out before her. Empty, vacant of any goal or dream. She longed to believe she had Elias, but he was elsewhere, doing something that didn't involve her. And there was everything right with that. Could she do the same thing?

The idea of going back to school flitted through her head. She reflexively batted it away. It was ridiculous to think of a woman her age going back to school, or even getting her high school diploma now. There was no point. It was a waste of time. Her eyes drifted over Elias's bookcase. In all honesty, reading was a struggle for her. There had been a time, as a kid, she had occupied libraries and read voraciously. They were safe places to be. Still were, but as she grew older and more streeted, she felt too much shame to take herself into them anymore. Like a filthy sinner walking into a church, places of learning and knowledge weren't for those that had no hope of trying to better themselves.

Eyes still on the bookshelf, Margaret's thoughts traveled up two floors above her to Raymond's library, waiting and unused. It had been a sacred place to her. She recognized that now. And he had been Elias's last...whatever. A worded man. A man with purpose, all the way to the end of his life. A man who had obviously lived a real life and understood how to share that with someone else.

She headed back into the bathroom, where she went to the mirror. Yup, still old, still ugly. But today she had a purpose that forced her to look at the foul thing. Slowly, she opened her mouth and stuck her fingers inside. Three more dead teeth came out with very little coaxing or pain or blood, only a sense of relief as each popped free. Five more were loose. Maybe tomorrow. She didn't want to hurt herself more than she had to. As she examined her mouth again, she saw that in the spaces where the teeth had been, white buds were pushing through. Not only that, but spaces where teeth had fallen out long before budded with gleaming, white enamel.

As she moved her lips about with her fingers, she noticed another change. The nails on her fingers were *growing*. Smooth, healthy pinkness was replacing the cloudy, cracked talons she had stared at for the last couple of decades. Picking up Elias's nail clipper, she trimmed the tips, cutting away more of the old nails so the new now made up the majority. Another week like this and the worse of it would be gone altogether. Smiling down at her nails, she thought them almost pretty...

Still doesn't feel right, does it?

Margaret's eyes went round in the mirror.

"You can't be here."

You are such an idiot.

"No, you can't be here," she repeated. "This place is safe. I'm safe here."

It was, until you came here. Stupid woman. I am everywhere you are, you brought me with you.

"Well, then, get out. I don't want you..."

It feels the same, doesn't it? You feel exactly the same as you did yesterday. Nothing has changed.

"Stop. Don't do this."

He didn't save you, did he?

Margaret scooped up the brown teeth from where she had dropped them in the sink. "No, he is! He is saving me! Look."

And what are you doing for him? That made Margaret pause. *You see, he's got you so entranced, you've even stopped asking the questions. The questions you should be asking. Come on, Margaret, you've seen this all before. No one gives without wanting something. And when they think they have what they want, they quit trying. They show you their real faces. And the one he wears every day is so very pretty. Very unlike...*

Margaret stared at herself in the mirror. She saw scars and burns amongst her wrinkles that gave proof to what the darkness inside her said. She blocked it out.

You really going to close your eyes to it? Think that'll solve anything?

"I'll never look in a mirror again."

Ha. You've tried that before.

"He's not dark and twisted like me..."

He's exactly like you. She snapped her eyes open again as the truth of that statement twanged inside her. Without any idea why, she knew it was true. It was something she couldn't quite see, something just outside of her vision. The darkness chuckled with cruel satisfaction. *I'm always right, aren't I? You never believe me. Go ahead. Just watch and see. He'll show you the truth soon. They always do.*

Margaret turned away from the mirror and left the bathroom, the dark laughter echoing in her ears. She slammed the door and it seemed to cut the sound of it off. But in the distance, always in the distance, there was a soft sound of a baby crying. Crying desperately for her to...

Once she was dressed, she went back to the secret doors but paused. While Elias had said she was welcome to explore, it still felt unsettling to go back into the dead man's shrine and start using his things. She no longer really had an urge to go explore Raymond's library. Books no longer seemed like the haven they had been. More like a honey trap.

The problem with honey traps is there was a reason they worked.

Mounting the stairs going up, her apprehensions stayed in the apartment below her. She quickly found herself back on the third floor facing the hallway and its four doors. She moved at first to go toward Raymond's door, only to hesitate as she looked at the others. Each was also fitted with a nameplate. She went to the one across from Raymond's place instead.

The nameplate was blank.

Furrowing her eyebrows, Margaret reached for the handle. It opened easily, creaking inward with a hollow sound. On the other side lay a darkened room. Flipping the light switch, there was a hesitant flicker, then an overhead light came on, revealing a somewhat dusty twin to Raymond's apartment. Other than that, it was empty. No furniture, no furnishings. She didn't even bother going in to see the kitchen or the other bedroom, shutting off the light and closing the door instead. Leaving her fingers on the handle, she stared at the blank plate. With her other hand, she traced over the smooth, cool metal imagining her name scrawled there.

Like Raymond's.

Like who else?

Turning down the hall, she moved to the next door on the same side. It, too, had a plate, this one with elegant scrawling.

Zachariah's Room.

She stared at the plate. It was as polished as Raymond's, yet it seemed older. A few more tiny nicks. Slightly different metal composition.

She grasped the handle of the door and turned. It, too, was unlocked, but the turn was clunky and obviously needed some WD-40. The hinges creaked as she pushed the door inward. This room was clearly not empty, but it was oppressively dark. She tried to switch on the lights, but her fingers only came across a round object. After some questing and cursing, she realized it needed to turn. There was a loud snap as the lights in the room came on. Margaret's eyes went wide.

Like the empty, spare room, this one was coated in dust. She tasted it on the air it was so thick. The furniture in this room was covered with large light-colored sheets. The whole place looked like an inanimate object ghost party. The floor plan was much the same as the other two apartments, but that was where the similarities ended.

Stepping into the room felt like stepping back in time. The walls were covered in a fine, light-colored wallpaper stenciled with elegant fleur-de-lis in a slightly lighter shade. A large mirror hung above the ghost shape of a sofa, layered in dust so thick it didn't reflect anything in the room, but the frame was elegant and gold-colored. Like something out of the *Great Gatsby*. A wooden cabinet, filled the wall opposite the couch, ending where the kitchen began. It, too, was made of elegantly carved wood. By the indents, panes of glass lay behind the thick layer of dust coating the cabinet. A pooled sheet lay before it and Margaret could only conclude that at some point, the sheet had slipped off, failing in its duty to protect the cabinet.

Unable to resist, Margaret went to the cabinet and rubbed at one of the panes of glass. On the other side, were toys. Old and worn and clearly loved by a child of some time long gone. Her heart began to beat faster and she found it hard to catch her breath. She remembered toys from another time, created in an era not so long ago, carefully collected for another child, never to be played with. She focused on the objects and tried to forget what they represented. These were not the same as those, and yet easily recognizable. There was a small, rough-edged wooden cart with a little carved driver holding a whip. The horses were missing from the traces. Next to the cart sat a little tin man with a round hat, 'sitting' in a green metal boat. Or rather the lower half of his body was the boat and two oars stuck out from his hands. A large wind-up key stuck out from his prow. Also on the shelf were a cluster of small sheep figures, both standing and laying down, stared on with painted red eyes. One of them lay stiffly on its side, its broken-off leg next to it. Margaret's heart ached for this child long gone, never to play with these sad, lost toys again. She shuddered and looked away, haunted by the ghost of a child's laughter.

She glanced at the other objects in the cabinet. An ornate globe sat to the right of the toys, resting on a brass-looking pedestal. Another section held different pairs of eyeglasses, each looking more uncomfortable to wear than the last. They were all about the same size, only changing in material and shape as if worn through the decades of a lifetime. Several pocket watches were also laid out on a dusty square of dark blue velvet. Opening one of the drawers beneath, she found them stuffed with packets of letters, bound up with waxed twine. There were several drawers of them. Lifting out one packet, she stared down at the scrawled writing and faded postmarks with a small black and white stamp of a man in a cravat, the number "22" printed at the lowermost corner.

"Elias," she whispered. The handwriting matched that on the plaque marking the door to the apartment. The name written in the middle of the envelope was in the same handwriting. Margaret frowned. The thick twine obscured the last name. When she tried to slip her newly growing fingernail under to try to lift it up and read, the packet of letters began to crumble and crack almost too loudly for paper. Alarmed, she dropped the pages back into their drawer and didn't dare pick them back up again. Her heart pounding, she turned away and moved farther into the room.

Her eyes went wide at the sight of the kitchen. It was the same size as Raymond's had been, but there were no modern appliances whatsoever. Instead, sitting against the wall, was a large, black, square, iron monstrosity looking like something straight out of Little House on the Prairie. Black iron pans hung above it, each covered by a small pile of dust. A series of planks were set into the wall, running from floor to ceiling. Porcelain dishes stood upright on the shelves, held in place by an inset edge to keep them that way. One dish hadn't stayed in place, however. It had crashed to the tiled floor long ago, the shards now lost under the layered dust. There was no sink, but an old wash bin sat under the window on a small bench that extended far enough for a small stack of thin towels to wait for nobody beside it. Heavy burnt-gold-colored curtains still hung in the windows, stained with age.

Margaret's heart was still beating hard, though she couldn't put a finger on why. What was this place?

Pressure built behind her eyes and she pressed against her temple, but it did little to relieve it. On the edge of her hearing, she thought she heard laughter, a child's laughter. Spinning around, she focused all her attention on the sounds in the silent room. There was nothing.

Needing some kind of answer, she went to the door, but again the hallway held nothing and no one.

"Must have been kids on the street," she muttered and for half a beat she almost returned to the hallway. Instead, she turned back and went straight to the opposite wall, surprising herself. Then she heard it again, the joyful, childish laughter coming from behind a draped sheet on the wall. Seizing it in her hands, she pulled harder than she needed; the sheet fell away easily.

Her palpating heart nearly stopped in shock.

A painting of a woman and child hung on the wall before her. The woman's face seemed sweetly angelic, framed by sable hair pinned up in curls that draped elegantly around her neck. Her deep dark brown eyes smiled wickedly, while her mouth seemingly tried to maintain a dignified line but lost the battle. She wore a simple, silvery gown and a black lace shawl over her shoulders, the style looking like something a woman would wear around the time the founding fathers were building the nation.

Beside her stood a boy, maybe eight years old. Like the woman, his eyes and hair were brown, making it very obvious that she was his mother. He also wore grey, with some sort of white lace collar around his shoulders and neck. Unlike his mother, though, his expression came across as sweet and clearly innocent. His features were different from his mother's, but it was clear he would grow up just as striking in appearance.

The two figures held hands as they waited during their portrait sitting. There wasn't much else in the painting other than a backdrop curtain and an open window showing a small scene of water and shoreline beyond.

Margaret stopped her fingers mere inches from the face of the small child. She ached inside at the sight of him.

"Who are you?" she asked the figure, but no answers came from the still image.

Feeling supremely uncomfortable, Margaret picked up the sheet and attempted to cover the painting again. Yet, once uncovered, the painting wouldn't go back beneath its shroud and she had to give up.

She better tell Elias about her snooping and get his help replacing the sheet. Hopefully, he was done with his special client.

Leaving Zachariah's room was a great relief, as if she had been leaving a room of mourning, and she hurried down the hall to get as far away as she could. Quietly, she slipped down the steps, feeling better as she passed down each set.

When she neared the ground floor, she again heard the distinct sound of laughter. This time a *woman's* tinkling laugh. That stopped her cold.

After a few moments, the laughter died down and low conversation took its place. Edging down the last few steps, Margaret peeked through the door, which stood ajar.

Warm, streaking sunlight poured in through the large windows in the front of the shop, dancing with dust particles. At first, all seemed still, then a shift of movement caught her eye. Against the far wall, a ladder slid along a row of shelves on a small track, resting about two-thirds of the way from the nearest end. The back of Elias's head appeared as he rose up the rungs. As he reached for a shoebox-sized container, he continued to speak softly to someone below just to his left.

Margaret slid into the room, and as quietly as possible, tried to edge her way to the end of the aisle to peek around the corner at Elias's guest.

She was a beautiful woman. Naturally. The woman's dark skin was dressed in a riot of sunshine that made her glow a warm, soft brown. It was like she held the essence of the sun itself within her. Compared to Elias, she appeared older, with the elegant agedness of a queen. Her dark coils were piled on the top of her head like an artist had placed them there. Her entire being moved with joy.

Margaret hated the sight of her.

Elias turned himself around on his ladder, so his lithe body faced her, resting against the slightly steeped rungs as he opened the box. Together, in the eclectic space, they looked like a photo shoot for a magazine but with no photographer to capture the money shot. Just an old woman spying, still trying to slide closer, moving along the other side of the aisle to hear their words better.

"How many geodes do you think you'll need?" Elias asked, looking up from the box.

"How many do you have?" the beautiful woman asked.

His eyebrows shot up as he looked back into the box, shifting the contents inside with a finger. He seemed to be counting softly to himself as the rocks inside clacked against each other when they moved.

"Six complete, twice as many halves," he responded.

"How much for all of them?" The beautiful woman's expression remained serene and neutral, as if she asked the most natural thing in the world. Based on Elias's reaction, it wasn't.

Cocking his head a bit to the side in a way that Margaret recognized as his tell that he was intrigued, he shook the box a little again, resettling the contents before popping the top back on.

"What's going on, Lady Ursula?" He stepped down the ladder the rest of the way to the ground, letting gravity take him the last couple of steps. His eyes never left the woman's face and she met his gaze the whole way down.

After another tense moment of studying each other, the beautiful woman quirked a small smile. "Are you saying you want to get involved again?" she asked instead of answering.

At that, Elias turned away and headed to the end of the aisle. The end where Margaret hid. Panicked, she tried not to be too obvious as she scuttled into the middle of the aisle, passing them the opposite way as the beautiful woman followed where Elias led.

"Excellent dodge," Elias called as he reached the end of the aisle and strolled past.

"I could say the same for you," the beautiful woman replied as she followed. Neither looked toward where Margaret squatted a few feet away. Instead, they moved to Elias's counter. Margaret decided to press her luck and paralleled them until she squatted beside a table display that gave her cover and a good view of the counter. In the back of her thoughts, she marveled at how she was able to squat as she hadn't for ages, but most of her focus was on what was being said a few feet away.

"You are the politician, not I." Elias stepped behind his counter and set the box down in the middle of the space. Then he bent down and retrieved an old-fashioned balance scale along and a second, smaller wood box.

"Indeed, and I regret it every day." The beautiful woman set her hands on the opposing side of the counter, folding them neatly on top as she watched Elias open the smaller box. Carefully, he hooked out three weights by their looped ends and set them on one plate of the scale, which immediately dropped.

"I won't sell you the whole box because I can't get these too easily anymore since the trade war with China began. I can think of about a dozen reasons to need these, but only two that might require so many." He raised an eyebrow at his guest.

"I need to calm a mind," she conceded. He continued to wait. "She was touched by the Oberon and the Faerie Court."

Elias nodded at that. He added another, larger weight to the scale. From the other box, he removed a symmetrical brown rock and set it exactly in the middle of the empty plate. "Exactly how old? Or rather..." he shrugged, "not exactly. Give me within five years."

"I am estimating very late twenties, maybe just turned thirty."

He returned a rock he had just selected to the box and removed a different one instead. This one was a partial piece, and Margaret glimpsed the crystallized insides glinting with a wink of light, flashing blood red. He continued to pile pieces of geode onto the scale along with three whole ones until the weights were balanced. After the plates settled, he studied the scale, then nodded and stretched out a hand from his side and snapped. There was a cracking sound, followed by the *ting* of metal impacting metal. Then a key flew into Elias's hand, his fingers closing around it with abnormal speed.

The beautiful woman's eyes went slightly wider. Elias smirked. He bent down behind his counter and used the key. Margaret couldn't see what he was doing, but she heard a sliding sound before he reappeared and set another box on the counter. This one was perfectly cubed and made of dark, ornate wood that had been elaborately carved. Elias set his hands on either side of the box, squaring up behind it as if preparing to duel.

"I will sell you the geodes, but this—" he tapped the box with his fingertips, "is only on loan, in exchange for a favor."

The beautiful woman narrowed her eyes at him. "I do not need the Souls Box to perform the ritual."

"But it'll be a lot safer if you use it."

She studied the box a moment with a slight tilt of her head. "What is the favor?"

"Do you accept?"

"It depends on what the favor is. And whether it involves me personally or the Chair of the Inner Council."

Elias's smile deepened. "My Lady's Wizard's challenge with that boy, Abraxas, is coming up."

"He's more than a boy. He's a journeyman wizard in his own right."

"He is a boy," Elias assured.

"And I will do nothing to interfere with that. It was a legal challenge." She met his eye.

"And I'm not asking you to. I believe my Lady will rise to the challenge herself without the Inner Council's support…"

"Then what do you want from me?"

"…But the duel would be a lot safer with it," Elias finished.

Margaret's head was spinning. She had no idea what they were talking about. Who was this Lady they kept referring to? And what were the geodes for? She would have thought they were just dirty rocks, but apparently held hidden value. What else on these shelves was ugly but worth more on the inside?

The beautiful woman shifted her stance. "There is another favor I would much rather offer you." She leaned in, setting her hand over his. "I could make you your own House."

Elias withdrew sharply. "I have already sworn to my Lady and passed on my claim."

"I do not mean the House of the Magdalene. I speak of your own House, Elias. You have more than a right to create one."

"No." He moved back and started dumping the geodes off the plate onto the counter, letting the opposing plate crash, its burden also rolling onto the counter. He proceeded to angrily return his weights to their box.

"We need you, Elias. Maybe you're right, and Rune manages to hold onto Maddie's legacy. All well and good, but these are dark times for us all. We need you. We need strength and for *all* of our members, our people, to engage in the fight."

"I am not one of your people," he snapped. "And I will not participate in another war."

The beautiful woman blinked. She seemed a bit stunned but said nothing more. Margaret watched Elias's ire crumpled a little as he slowed his too-fast-clean-up. "I apologize. That was unfair." He sighed and looked in Margaret's direction. In reaction, she ducked back down behind the table, her heart pounding, certain he saw her.

"I understand, your position," he continued, as if maybe he hadn't, "I do. But I will have to insist that my answer is no. I will continue on the course I have chosen."

Since he wasn't going to call her out, Margaret edged back up to keep spying.

He set his hand on the ornate box again. "Do you want the box or not?"

The beautiful woman searched his face for a long breath, but then she deliberately reached out and pulled Elias's box toward her. "I'll take the geodes in a box if you have it?"

"Of course, my Lady Ursula," Elias said with a small upper body bow, his open hands spread apart over the counter.

The beautiful woman...Lady Ursula sighed as she drew elegant gloves over her long, articulate fingers. "I really should know better than to make deals with one of your kind," she admonished herself with a renewed lovely smile.

They continued to banter, using many words to say very little as Elias boxed up the geodes, then wrapped the ornate box in silky red cloth and placed it in a second plastic container.

Margaret's legs and back started to cramp. Just as she made up her mind to try to crawl back down the aisle, Elias straightened. "That will be thirty thousand in total."

The old woman practically fell over with shock. Thirty thousand *dollars*? Neither of those she spied on seemed to think that amount excessive. In fact, Lady Ursula seemed to expect it. She withdrew a too-thin envelope from her pocket and pressed it into Elias's hand. He didn't open it; just slipped it into his back pants pocket as she picked up her packages.

He came around his counter and escorted her to the door.

Now, Margaret shifted back, moving deeper into the aisle. Once they approached the door, Elias moved to open it for the Lady. They exchanged a few more words and a pair of kisses on each other's cheeks before the beautiful woman exited. Gently, Elias shut the door and locked it, flipping the open sign to closed and pulling down the shade over the glass door. Margaret straightened up, debating with herself about whether she should try to escape or wait for him to turn. She was so sure that he had seen her when he had glanced over that she was shocked when he turned and jumped out of his skin at the sight of her.

"Geez!" he cried, grabbing at his chest as if he feared his heart was going to leap out. "Were you hiding there the whole time?"

"I thought...I thought you saw me." Internally, she kicked herself. She could have escaped with him none the wiser.

"I..." He leaned back against the door. "No. No, I didn't. Man. You almost gave me a heart attack."

"I doubt that," Margaret countered under her breath. She opened her mouth to say something defensive, something to deflect what would be a justified censor for spying. Instead, she took in Elias, leaning hard against the door. His eyes drifted, not seeing anything, like he was far, far away. "Elias?"

Soul came back into his eyes and he smiled back at her.

"You look like an angel," he said softly.

Margaret touched her hair. Denial rolled through her body, even if she wouldn't let it come out of her mouth this time. She was trying to be better about that.

"Do...do you need a hug?" she asked, her cheeks burning. She held out her arms to him, but couldn't meet his eyes, only glance at them sideways.

Deliberately, he peeled himself off the door. His hips swayed a little bit as he prowled—and prowled was definitely the word for it—toward her. Grunting softly, Margaret stepped forward, covering the rest of the space that he took his dear, sweet time crossing. Putting her arms around his neck was a bit awkward, as he was taller than her and she had to reach for him. She stood stiff, staring straight ahead over his shoulder, like a soldier enduring a battle. Slowly, his own arms came around her and she started counting in her head. Was ten seconds long enough? Did he need twenty? Thirty?

Then, his weight began to settle onto her as he let go of himself. His forehead drifted down and, with a great, exhausted sigh, he pressed his face into the crook of her neck. It stopped being about requirements and time. His warmth surrounded her, penetrating her to her bones. And she wanted to be there. She began to squeeze him for all she was worth, as if to say 'I understand.' It didn't matter what she understood. She simply did. He cupped her head with his hand, firmly and tenderly. He understood back.

"Who was that woman?" she asked, her question rolling through their chests as she murmured it.

She felt him tense, but she held on.

"The outside world. The past is trying to eat the future."

Margaret tried to pull back to look in his face, but he clung harder. "What?"

"I don't want to talk about her."

"Elias."

"You smell nice."

This time she managed to push herself free. "Elias..."

"Let's go get your hair cut. Would you like that?"

CHAPTER 7

"SHARON WILL BE TAKING CARE OF YOU IN THE BACK," THE MIDDLE-AGED receptionist said, giving them both a practiced smile.

Hearing her name, the blonde hairdresser perked up and turned to look straight at Elias, who looked stunningly handsome in a charcoal grey jacket over a soft, black t-shirt and black skinny jeans. He wore a leather string as a necklace and the shades he had popped up on top of his head made him look like he was ready for a photo shoot instead of taking someone to a hairdresser. Margaret hated the way the perky young blonde's face lit up at the sight of him, her hand already extended, presumably to shake his, or maybe grab him and run off to bed with him. Margaret's seething rage got sharper when the receptionist stood up and introduced her as the client, and Perky Sharon's face drooped for a half a second in disappointment before jumping back into a professional smile.

"Margaret, nice to meet you," she said, belatedly offering her hand to her actual client.

"I'll bet," Margaret retorted, staring down the hand she had no intention of taking. Sharon lowered it, unsure, struggling to keep that smile on her face, to Margaret's wicked delight.

"Margaret," Elias chided with a gentle warning. *His* smile never wavered, just became that priestly serene thing on his face.

Immediately, Margaret felt chagrined. "My apologies," she muttered and tried to reach out and shake, which made an awkwardly uncoordinated effort for both of them.

"Come with me," Sharon recovered first, and led them both to a work station in the middle of a row of shiny, swivel chairs. Margaret kept her eyes forward, trying to endure the facing mirrors that reflected back infinite identical versions of her, an old woman dressed in jeans with an elastic band and an oversized grey sweater with pink embroidery on the front that read the lie 'World's Best Grandma.' She had wanted to drop kick Elias when he brought it to her, but her salvation depended on changing her ways, so she had grimaced a smile.

Sharon settled the "World's Best Grandma" in her chair.

"Hey, Margaret," Elias called gently. She shifted her gaze a little to the left. He had taken a seat in a plain, white chair right next to the mirror. "Don't look there, look here," he said, pointing to his eyes. "I am your mirror."

She couldn't help herself, she returned his smile with a smaller, reluctant one of her own.

"Is your grandson taking you out on a date today?" Sharon asked as she brought around a hairdresser's cape in front of Margaret's vision, before attaching it under her long, uneven white hair at the back of her neck.

"Yes, this is a date," Elias answered before Margaret could.

"Lucky grandma, having such a handsome grandson to take you around the town," Sharon said in a cutesy voice that set Margaret's teeth on edge.

"Now, what do we want to do with your hair?" the hairdresser asked, catting her fingers through it. "Oh my, it's so soft."

"Just cut it nice," Margaret said, through gritted teeth, trying to be civil in front of Elias.

"How about something like this?" Elias asked, holding up a magazine she hadn't seen him pick up. He had obviously been thumbing through it because he was about halfway in. The model in the picture showed off a hairstyle that was close to a 1950s bob, the hair stopping at about her chin and tapering up a little bit toward the back.

Margaret narrowed her eyes at Elias in irritation. "That's a young woman's haircut, I would look silly."

"Oh, I don't know, I think your grandson here has excellent taste." Sharon batted her eyes flirtatiously at him as she said it. Margaret doubted that was a genuine, professional opinion.

"Will you stop flirting with him and pay attention to me," Margaret snapped before she could swallow it.

"Uh oh, I think your grandmother is getting a little jealous," Sharon laughed and Margaret about slapped her.

"That's probably because you keep calling her my grandmother," Elias said, as he leaned an elbow onto the chair's arm and hooked one of his black-booted ankles over the opposite knee, looking even more like an out-of-place rock star.

Sharon kept her mask in place with some effort as she started to spray down the top of Margaret's hair with a mist of water. "Uh? What do you mean? She's not your grandmother?"

"Nope, she's not," Elias said, enjoying being unhelpful.

"So, what is this then, a senior citizen-outreach sort of thing?" she asked, picking up a comb and scraping it painfully over Margaret's head as she continued to ignore her and talk to Elias.

"Stop it! That hurts," Margaret snapped again.

"Oh, sorry, sweetie. I'm not trying to hurt you. No ouchies, I promise."

Margaret gripped the armrests with white-knuckled fingers and shot another look at Elias, begging him with her eyes for permission to let this bimbo have it.

He didn't look back at her but, instead, kept a steady gaze on the pretty, young thing, with her piled-high bun of rich blonde hair and the smart, tight-fitting hairdresser's smock. It almost broke Margaret's heart; she was so jealous.

"So, is this an outreach thing?" Sharon continued to probe as she combed more gently.

"No, it's more of a girlfriend-thing, I think." Sharon's hand slipped and the comb clattered to the ground, but it didn't stop Elias from speaking one bit. "I mean, I'm hoping so. We're taking things slow right now. But I think it's going very well." And the cheeky bastard winked.

"Oh...oh...I see..." Sharon twittered a nervous laugh as she tried to compose herself. "You're having me on? A joke?"

"No, no. No joke. I think she might be the love of my life," he said confidently.

"Elias," Margaret chided, turning away to hide her blush, which just made things harder on poor Sharon.

"Oh, okay. So, how are we cutting this then? I could shear it down real short?" she offered, using every ounce of professionalism she had.

"Do what he wanted," Margaret said, not looking at the "he" in question, but waving a dismissive hand at Elias.

"The bob?" Sharon asked, surprised.

"Yes, cut it like that," Margaret confirmed and closed her eyes so she didn't have to look at the mirror or Elias's smugly pleased expression.

A half an hour later, she opened them.

The woman looking back at Margaret was different. She seemed to be surprised, almost mesmerized by what was before her. She was still old, but somehow the age sat on her like an elegant mantle instead of smothering her features. Her neck was long, rising out of the still boney shoulders, and it rose even more as the woman sat up straighter, free from the weight of dead hair. Now it cascaded around each side of her face in soft waves of white that ended about her chin. The woman mirrored… Margaret's actions as she reached up with her fingers and touched the ends with reverence, letting them drink in the change, the shorter length, the new space underneath where hair had once been.

"What do you think?" the Sharon in the mirror asked.

"It's fine," Margaret conceded and started pulling at the cape, wanting it gone so she could get up. Sharon attempted to help her, but Margaret slapped her fingers away. The teeny-bopper's "help" wasn't getting her out of the cape any faster. Then Elias appeared over her shoulder. With two quick snap sounds, he had her free, whisking the cape gallantly to the side, taking the bits of hair clinging with it. Sharon scurried over to take it as Margaret tried to escape, wanting to run completely out of the shop. But before she could get far, Elias caught her hand. With a gallant spin, he turned her back to the mirror, cupping her in his arms.

"Let me go!" Margaret hissed, just as he brought his cheek down parallel with hers.

"Look," he whispered.

"I've already seen it," she dismissed, pitching her voice down to match his.

"Look at us," he insisted.

Realizing it was just easier to do as he asked, she shifted her eyes up to the stupid mirror. Immediately, her eyes went to Elias. The smile on his face was sinfully angelic. "We look like a magazine cover."

"Which one, Grandmother Weekly?"

He chuckled against her back. "You're right. Just a couple of old geezers living it up."

She met his gaze in the mirror, older than her own despite the lack of age lines. She couldn't help it, she had to smile back.

"Let's find you something a little foxier to wear..." mirror Elias said.

"Elias..." she barely got out before he seized her hand again.

"Your hair looks wonderful," the receptionist said, as Elias paused to hand her a couple of bills.

"Thank—" Margaret barely got out before they were off again, out the door, its bells chiming harshly as if the door itself objected to being yanked with such force.

"Come on, this way," Elias urged as he turned down an alley.

"Where are we..." she started to ask before he turned again, walking them straight through a brick wall. Or at least, that was what she first thought he had done. It had happened so fast that Margaret didn't have time to flinch before they were already through.

"Amazed?" Elias asked as he paused to let Margaret take in the space. She found herself standing in another alley of sorts. It was more like a tunnel that went back twenty feet, except the far end disappeared into darkness instead of properly ending at a wall or something. Which would mean that it cut straight through the building they had just exited from. The tunnel was entirely made of brick. In places, someone had gotten creative, making designs with pieces of brick every few feet. The light was dim in the alley tunnel and she could see no one, other than the two of them.

"Well?" he prompted.

"Not really. I've seen things like this before," she answered.

"I suppose you've seen more of the in-between places in Chicago than I realized. I find this is the best way to access my favorite places, no matter where they are," he conceded. He then renewed his grip on her hand, laced her fingers in between each of his. "This way."

Margaret tried to tug her hand back. While it was true that she had walked into places like this before, places that shouldn't have existed but did, every time she had walked into one she had retreated as quickly as possible. Strange things often happened in such spaces, unpredictable things, possibly dark things.

"Elias, where are you taking me?" This time he heeded her resistance, turning back to her but not releasing her hand.

"I thought we would get you a new dress to go with the new hair."

"What kind of dress could we find in a place like this?"

"Only the very best for my Love," he said, adding a brief bow to his statement. "Why do you still look troubled?"

"Because you are trouble," she answered. Predictably, he grinned a grin that spoke volumes of anecdotal evidence to that being true. Together, they started strolling down the tunnel again. "I don't want a dress. That just feels silly."

"Then what do you want? What would please you, my Love?"

She chuckled, starting to like the dramatic way he talked. *Maybe how about you, tied up in a bed. No shirt.* She suppressed a wicked smile. "None of your business."

He guffawed. "I actually think it's very much my business. It is the mission I set myself, in fact. To make you happy."

"Then you chose an impossible mission. No one can make anyone else be happy. It's a stupid fiction created to sell things."

He arched his eyebrows. "That is true. You are very wise."

"No, I'm old and jaded, and now I have a new haircut."

"And it looks very nice."

Gently, she ran her fingers through her hair. "Yeah, it does," she agreed, "but..."

She stopped herself, her eyes going wide as she realized what she had almost said. It was probably too late.

He stopped and waited for her to finish.

Instead, she felt like she was drowning in his patient gaze. The last thing she needed to do was tell him her pet theory about him. It was simply too embarrassing. Again, after a few moments, he threw her a life raft.

"We're almost there. Shall we keep going?" he asked, gesturing to the tunnel ahead.

She turned to look. She hadn't really noticed before, but the tunnel had changed while they had walked. It still sloped in a wide, gentle arch, but the mouth of the tunnel had disappeared from sight, leaving nothing but darkness at either end of the tunnel. They had walked much further than twenty feet as they talked, like the tunnel had gone on for twice that, the opposing ends disappearing into darkness. It felt like they were in their own pocket of reality with nothing existing before or behind. The idea sent a shiver down her spine.

Not that it was truly dark; quite the opposite. Every few feet black, wrought-iron street lamps topped with three glass balls glowed with a warm, diffused light giving the space dreamlike edges. She realized there were people around now. Not all of them were human, or hominal. They emerged from the darkness, chatting pleasantly with each other as they went by the other way. At one point, a small cafe appeared out of the dark. People sat at small outdoor tables, enjoying coffee and cake. Their conversation followed Margaret and Elias as they moved off even after the café was swallowed by the darkness. Other doors appeared and disappeared in the arch of the wall, made of quality glass and wood. Above the doors, signs stuck out, some with iconic symbols and others with words written in elegant script.

The sign hanging above the store that they finally stopped in front of bore a thread spool and needle crossed with a deep red rose. Elias gestured to the door in invitation but waited for her to decide, dress or no dress?

She blew out a dramatic sigh. "Well, if it will make you happy."

With full gallantry, the beautiful man seized the door handle. "Elias Leveau?"

Together they turned as an older man approached. It took a second for Margaret to realize he was a vampire. The man's beatific smile made it hard to miss the elongated canines as he extended his arms, seeking a hug.

The vampire was dressed in a soft, fawn-colored jacket and matching dress slacks that were perfect for late fall. He had a cane in one hand that crossed with his arms as the shorter man snared Elias into a hug and joyfully lifted him off the ground. Elias endured it all with his serene, indulging smile. At the apex of the enthusiastic greeting, Margaret caught the flick of the vampire's eyes as he noted her before he set Elias back down. Not fully releasing him, the vampire continued to ignore her presence as he extended his arms straight to tenderly look into Elias's face.

"Dear lord, I think it has been a year since I've seen you…"

"Probably," Elias answered.

There was a beat of silence as the two men regarded each other, smiling, but neither knowing what to say.

"So, what are you doing here?" the vampire finally asked, releasing Elias's shoulders to take his cane in both hands instead.

"Just doing some shopping, in my favorite hard-to-reach shop," Elias answered. He didn't look at Margaret, but the vampire's eyes again flitted to her. This time it was clear he was forming an opinion. One she probably wouldn't like.

"Well, then, why don't you join me," he offered familiarly, turning his back to Margaret as he gestured for Elias to come with him toward the fancy cafe.

"Thank you, but I'll have to pass." Elias held up his hand.

"Elias," the vampire playfully chided, "you're going to make me beg? I haven't seen you in ages. I think we should catch up."

"Please don't make me be rude about it," Elias warned softly.

The vampire's face faltered but resisted a total collapse. He shot another glance at Margaret but continued to refuse to acknowledge her by Elias's side. Instead, he fiddled with his cane before he stepped in closer one last time.

"I miss you," he said in a low, alarmingly intense voice. "I miss us." The vampire's hands visibly shook as he gripped the cane. "I know...I know what I did was..."

"Martel," Elias finally laid a hand on the vampire's shoulder. "We don't need to dredge it up, but I am out now with my friend here."

"But, Elias..."

"We both know that we are not the best for each other. We both agreed." Elias's voice took on a sliver of warning that this time the vampire heeded.

His expression hardened even as he forced the congeniality back on his face. "Well, if a cup of coffee is too hard for you right now, maybe next time."

Elias nodded. "It was good to see you, Martel. Good luck with everything."

The nod was returned with less grace before the vampire turned on his heel and walked off.

Only after he had disappeared into the coffee shop did Elias turn back to Margaret.

"I'm sorry about..."

"What the hell was that?"

Elias double blinked, genuinely caught off-guard. "I... uh..."

She wasn't going to let him off the hook, staring quietly as he wriggled. Finally, he huffed. "I'm two hundred and fifty years-ish old, like I've said. I've been with a lot of different people."

"What the hell is that supposed to mean?"

"What I said. I believe in love; that understandings and companionship can come from anywhere. In my experience, it has."

Margaret snorted. She understood the subtlety of his statement, but she didn't want to. Still, she felt put out, though she couldn't put her finger on why.

"And he was your ex?"

"He was a mistake. Even I make them, though not very often."

"Oh, really?" Margaret set her fists on her hips. "And what, pray tell, made him a mistake?"

"Raymond had just died..." he huffed again and crossed his arms. "Margaret, I don't want to lie to you, and if you push it, I will answer, but I would rather buy you a dress and enjoy our night."

She blew out her own breath. What little he had said was enough for her to understand. "Fine. Fine. Buy me a pretty dress."

They turned back to the clothing store's door.

"So, do I make a complete set then? You haven't had an old lady yet?" she jibbed under her breath, not expecting an answer as she let herself be ushered into the store.

Not a store. A shop.

The air smelled of refinement and money, where clothes were measured to fit and everything was one-of-a-kind. The woman running the shop even greeted Elias with open arms that led to kisses on both cheeks.

"Elias, my lovely boy! It's been ages!" the beautiful woman, another beautiful woman, declared before turning to Margaret, her immaculate chocolate hair bouncing around her face. "And who is this?"

Before Margaret could say anything, the woman's dark eyes went up and down, followed by her whipping out a pair of thick-rimmed glasses that did not deter from the raging elegance of her look, but only added a veneer of hot-to-trot professional.

"Ah, I see, I see. Yes," she muttered, though Margaret had no idea what she was apparently "seeing" other than an old lady in frumpy clothes. "The hair is perfect, by the way. A very bold look." Then the beautiful woman turned and snapped twice in the air. "Maria, Latrisha, the fall collection, immediately! Elias! Bring your Silver Vixen this way."

"Come, my Love," Elias said, offering her his arm.

"Elias, what's going on?" Margaret demanded, even as she tentatively took it.

"Rosaleen is the best," he tried to assure her, failing as he led her through a pair of French-style doors into a private fitting and changing room in the back. "And don't worry. You can't insult her. She's impervious to it. Be as cranky as you like."

"I'm not cranky," she cranked, just in time to come face to face with two females, one hominal with the darkest ebony skin she had ever seen and the other a white fluffy Catwoman. They eyed her up and down before their boss, Rosaleen, clapped her hands together twice. "Come, come. At once!" she declared.

"Good. I like a challenge," the ebony woman said, and they both parted to gesture Margaret toward a dais.

Margaret eyed it like it was a sacrificial altar. "You're kidding."

"If you don't want to go on the dais, tell them," Elias said, and then he left her, taking a seat on a cushy chair positioned to the side. A flute of something pale yellow and bubbly waited for him on a side table. He plucked it up as he crossed his legs. While he took a healthy sip, he waggled his eyebrows at her playfully. She was on her own here, and he was laughing at her. She sighed, no he wasn't laughing, at least not at her. He seemed more excited.

She turned back to the waiting...whatever they were, shop girls? Seamstresses? The Catwoman pulled a measuring tape from the small kit sitting on a nearby stand, along with a wrist cushion already bursting with various pins like a porcupine's back. The ebony woman waited patiently for Margaret to comply with her request, completely unfazed by her dallying.

So. What did she want to do?

With an indulging sigh, Margaret mounted the velvet-covered dais and faced the trio of mirrors in front of it. Almost automatically, she clasped her hands in front of her and waited.

"I see you've been measured before," the white Catwoman purred as she approached, feeding out the tape from between the elongated toes of her upper paws, which really looked more like hands. A real cat, a small tabby with an extra-long tail, entered the dressing room, rubbing up along the glass in a show of elegant indifference.

"Would you care for anything to eat or drink?" the ebony woman asked.

"Like what?"

"Whatever you like," she said simply.

"Coffee," Margaret answered and continued waiting. "Just straight, black coffee."

The ebony woman nodded once and turned, leaving the room by a side door made to look like a part of the wall.

After that, Margaret settled in and let the Catwoman measure every part of her, noticing she never wrote anything down. Not that it really bothered Margaret. It wasn't her problem to remember her measurements. She certainly didn't know them now.

What did bother her were Elias's eyes. They never looked away as her measurements were taken. Though a small stack of magazines sat on the side table, he ignored them, completely content to watch.

"Do you wish me to ask the gentleman to leave?" the Catwoman asked as she rose, looping the measuring tape over her head.

"No, he's fine. Nothing he hasn't seen before." Margaret lowered her arms. "Are we done here?"

"Yes, Madame. You may undress at your convenience." The Catwoman bobbed her head once, respectfully, and then turned away as Rosaleen returned. The two females spoke softly to each other, ignoring their guests.

Margaret sighed and decided it was simpler to comply. The sooner this was over, the sooner she could get out of here. Before she had a chance to strip off her "Grandma" clothes, the ebony woman returned. Her tray offered a delicate cup on a saucer, wafting rich, fragrant coffee. Margaret took it, her mouth salivating at the scent.

"Take your time, Margaret," Rosaleen called and exited with the Catwoman on her heels. "Latrisha will assist you as need be."

"I don't need anyone's assistance," Margaret replied, laying that ground rule right then.

"As you wish," Latrisha answered and, unperturbed, turned to exit the room with her tray.

"You're doing well," Elias said before the door had fully closed.

"Why are we here, Elias?"

"I wanted to give you the royal treatment today," he answered, setting his nearly empty flute onto his side table.

"For heaven's sake, why? This is embarrassing." She took a sip of the coffee. Rich and dark and everything coffee should have always been. "Oh, my god. What is this?" she asked, before even trying to swallow down her mouthful, which resulted in a little dribbling onto the carpet.

"I imagine a Turkish blend of some sort. I can ask Rosaleen if you like."

Margaret downed the small cup in her second sip. "Oh. Oh, that's...that's..."

Elias laughed. "I daresay, I think you liked it."

"Don't get smug with me," Margaret said, but the snap just wasn't in her voice anymore. Instead, she found herself smirking, almost on the brink of laughing. "So, what exactly are you offering here? Anything I want? Keep it within a limit?"

"I would say, maybe pick out something fancy. I'm making an evening of this now." He ran a finger along his jawline. "If you like Turkish coffee, then maybe we need to try some other Turkish things."

She narrowed her eyes. "Like what?"

"It's a surprise."

She narrowed her eyes more.

"Don't trust me?"

"Absolutely not. I just haven't figured out how you're lying to me yet."

"I am an open book to you, my Love."

"Then who was that woman in your shop earlier?"

"The head of the Magic Guild." He responded so directly Margaret had to pause. He grinned at her owlish expression. "What?"

"I just realized that might be the first straightforward answer I've ever gotten from you."

"Am I lying?"

"Yes. Anyone who answers that plainly is hoping to hide a bigger truth behind the smaller, minimal one."

Now it was Elias's turn to look owlish and Margaret's to grin. "I see, she was a lover once?" Margaret added.

Elias swallowed his Adam's apple. "Not quite. Close."

"What happened?"

"She was looking for an 'ever after.'"

"She wanted to marry you?"

"She would have asked for it eventually, yes."

"Would that have been so bad?"

"I don't marry children."

That made Margaret pause to think about it. He had said he was a couple centuries old, basically immortal.

"By that logic, aren't I a child compared to you?"

"There's a big difference between someone at the beginning of their life and someone at the end."

Something gripped Margaret's stomach at that statement. "Well, I realize that I'm on death's door...."

"That wasn't intended to hurt you."

Margaret continued to glare.

He sighed and sat forward. "When you thought I was an elementary-something kid, you were very vocal against us being a couple of any kind. In fact, I know you are swallowing it back, but when you look at us together, it still makes you recoil a little, doesn't it? Just looking at this pretty face." He circled his said face with a finger.

The twist in Margaret's guts released a little. "I suppose so."

He captured her free hand to turn the knuckles to his lips, not kissing them but letting his lips whisper over as he spoke. "And why was that?"

"Because...because...but it is not the same. You've still got your life ahead of you, don't you? You may be old, but you're not dying."

At that, he did lay a thoughtful kiss on her hand, his eyes far, far away again. "While that may be true, I'm certainly not living either." He sat back, and for a moment Margaret saw the ancient man behind the young man's face.

"A young woman would want children and to build a life. I could give that to her, you're right, but it would be starting over again. No discovery, no adventure. And she would age and she would die and our children, most of them would likely age and die, all while I stayed like this. The other alternative is for me to leave before that happens. Then, I'm abandoning my family when they need me, because when are they going to stop needing me?" Finally, he raised his eyes to Margaret, who had stood as still as a statue, listening with no judgment. "I don't have the heart to try again."

"You were a father?"

"My son died several lifetimes ago, an old man with no issue. I was spared that at least."

"Zachariah?"

He nodded stiffly. "Did I already tell you about him?"

"No," Margaret admitted. "His name is on one of the nameplates in your hall." She thought about telling him about her excursion into the long-gone child's room but decided this wasn't the time.

"Why would I want more children to watch live and die? While I continue on? That would be my existence."

A heavy, tense silence hung over them for a moment. "I understand," she finally said, her voice barely breaking sound.

His expression hardened, tears making his eyes glitter brightly. "How? How could you possibly?"

Her hand slipped to the place over the small bulge of her abdomen, where she never properly healed and never would. "I killed my baby." The silence again hung heavy between them as he waited for more. "Now, you understand why I don't deserve your mercy." It felt both good and wrong to admit that out loud.

"Margaret."

"Don't. Don't do that. Don't pity me," she whispered, backing away, her voice breaking. She realized then his hand had wrapped around her wrist, tugging her gently.

"How did your baby die?"

"I was pregnant. I was doing all the wrong things. My husband was not a good man, but he was the best someone like me could expect...He..." her hands crossed over her abdomen. "We got into a fight. I was nagging him about not fixing the damn crib that I bought. I should have just left it alone or given Georgie the blow job he wanted to fix it for me. Anything else. He...he beat me so hard...I couldn't stop him..." She turned away, made to run. Elias's arms came around her, restraining her, and she panicked. "No, please."

"Margaret, it's okay."

"No, it's not. It can never be okay. It's bad enough that I don't even cry about it anymore. I used to sob at the slightest thought of her."

"The baby was a girl?"

"I don't know. It might have been. When I came awake, the nurses wouldn't let me see her. Said it was for the best. The bitch couldn't tell me what the baby's gender was, she hadn't bothered to look. But I wanted a girl."

In the distance, Margaret still heard her crying, though. Crying out for her to come, but no matter how far Margaret walked, she would never get any closer to her baby.

Instead, she turned away from Elias just as Latrisha and the Catwoman returned, pushing a rack with clothing swaying between them. Rosaleen reappeared behind them and clapped her hands twice.

"You are not undressed yet? Please, hurry, hurry! I have exactly the right thing for you."

Heedless of the woman's hand-flapping and mutterings, Margaret gracelessly pulled off her clothes in her own time. Elias said nothing, but she felt him watching. She knew she was supposed to take pleasure in this, getting dressed up in pretty clothes and being pampered, but it was all a useless exercise to her. She stepped up onto the velvety dais. Despite herself, she wiggled her wrinkled toes against the softness of the carpet. With much fanfare, Rosaleen poofed a dress before Margaret, the top open wide for her to step into. She did so without being told. The women drew the gown up, swathing her degraded self in rich, sumptuous black silkiness, the fabric whispering over her skin as the dress was cinched in the back. The two assistants buzzed around her, adjusting, pinning, stitching adjustments on the spot, talking softly to each other. Margaret never once looked up at the tri-fold mirrors she faced.

"What do you think, madam?" Rosaleen finally asked.

"It doesn't matter what I think. What does he think?" Margaret answered the floor, jerking a thumb in Elias's last known direction. She was surprised when his voice came from closer to her left.

"Rosaleen, will you please give us some privacy."

The pause was long and heavy enough that Margaret nearly glanced up.

Finally, Rosaleen spoke, her tone indulgent. "I need to run some errands. And I haven't treated my assistants in too long. Will an hour or two suffice?"

"I am indebted to you, Rosaleen, as always," Elias answered.

"Never, and you know that perfectly well." All three females left the room, shutting the double French doors behind them. A few moments later, Margaret heard the faint tinkle of bells, then silence.

"Had yourself a think, and changed your mind about this whole situation now that you know the truth?" Margaret challenged before he could say anything. She hadn't finished speaking when he stepped up onto the dais. His abrupt closeness forced a shocked breath into her and she snapped her head up to face him. Before she could stumble back, he had an arm around her waist.

"Do you want to forget?" he asked.

"What?" was the only question she could startle out.

"Say yes...." Gently he brushed his fingers through her hair. "Or no..."

Margaret shuddered. It felt like more than a mere brushing. When he did it again, she felt something akin to electric tingles wash over her skin, touching deeper than the surface.

"Do you want to forget the pain?" he asked, even more softly.

"No. I don't want to forget her," she answered just as softly.

"You won't. You can never forget her. There isn't enough magic in the world to make a mother forget her child, never truly forget. But I can take away the pain of the memory. Make it less immediate."

"No...I must feel it. I have to."

"Margaret, no amount of suffering will bring her back."

"But it wasn't fair, it wasn't right." She stared up at him, into his beautiful, angelic face. He understood. The tightness in her chest gripped around her pounding heart. "I should have died with her."

"She would have wanted you to live."

"And what have I done with that life? I waited too long."

He thumbed the edge of her chin. "May I kiss you?" he asked.

"I already said you could, didn't I?"

He stayed in place, so close their breaths mingled. When she finally couldn't stand it anymore, she closed the distance and kissed him instead. It was warm and soft and perfect, kissing as two people who really did know how to do the act well. And then she felt a tingle and knew what was happening. Magic seeped into her. Not through the kiss, but rather from the air all around them, sinking in past her clothes into her being. It held a question, asking her permission to enter.

At last, she allowed it in. It filled her with sunshine and shadow, warmth and chill. Sending her back until she found herself in that ill-fated hospital room, just opening her eyes.

The memory played out before her. Waking up. Calling for help. Searching desperately for any sign of her baby. The nurse coming in. The sharp words and quick slaps on her arms when she tried to get up. Being told what happened. Feeling like she was going to be sick and the sickness was a scream tearing through her.

And then it stopped only to start over again.

Over and over, the scene played. By the third time, Margaret became aware of a pulsing in her hands.

Elias's voice came from outside the memory. "Detach from what you see, as if you are but an observer."

"I can't..."

"Try."

The memory played again. And she did it, at least a little bit. The sensation felt like floating outside of herself, looking down on a young, sickly-looking woman. At first, she had only contempt for the image of herself, the disregard and disgust she had felt when her face had looked like...Margaret. It was the face she always expected to see when she looked in the mirror and was always shocked when the old woman stared back. Looking at that young face now, old Margaret wondered how she could ever have thought herself ugly. Young Margaret was tired and sick, but her hair was beautiful. Her bright eyes. Her clear skin. Her delicate hands.

Her daughter could have looked like this.

"What do you see?"

"She's so young."

"Yes. She is."

"I mean, she's a kid. Just a *kid* and..."

"And what?"

"She's so alone. A kid like that, someone should be here to..."

"It's okay, just say it."

"They should give her a hug. Tell her...tell her..."

"That it's not her fault?"

"No. That it doesn't matter whose fault it is. It just doesn't matter."

"What would you do for this young woman, if you were there right now?"

And then she was there. She was in the hospital room, looking down at the grieving young mother in the bed.

"I can't," old Margaret said. "No one ever hugged me. I'm too broken."

"Or you are broken enough. You understand."

"Yeah. Yeah, I understand." And then her arms clutched her younger self against her shoulder, feeling her cry and heave. "There, there. There, there," old Margaret cooed, brushing her hand down the back of young Margaret's messy hair. "It's going to be okay."

And then she held a smaller form. A child, crying hard. Her mother had slapped her, she had broken something important, but she hadn't meant to. "There, there. There, there, little girl. It's going to be okay. You're okay. You're just a little girl. You didn't know. You didn't mean to. It's going to be okay." How strange to feel comforted even as she gave comfort, living in both places at once, mother and child.

"Take a deep breath," the other voice said, gently, "and come back to me."

It took an eternity, but there was no rush. When Margaret managed to open her eyes, she blinked twice. Tears had rolled down her cheeks, but it felt good, clean. Gently, Elias pressed a handkerchief into her hand. She lifted it to dry her face, taking in a deep breath, deeper than any she had taken in decades.

"What did you do to me?" she asked. Elias had stepped down from the dais, his backside to the tri-fold of mirrors. It was a nice view from all three angles. She almost laughed at the observation.

"A little magic and some therapeutic technique. The human brain has the means to heal itself, once provided the right tools."

"I feel so different."

"You look different too," he said, and stepped to the side, out of the view of the mirrors.

In the glass stood a woman reflected in three different aspects. She stood tall, with wavy silver hair cut into a short elegant bob that made her look fresh and refined. She was obviously older but not worn away. A rich black dress hugged her figure in the right places, bringing dignity and grace to her form. As the dark fabric pooled down her body, she noticed small pieces of reflective silver glitter sparsely at first, then become denser as they descended to the edge of her skirt, like the tails of a comet crashing to earth. Bringing her hands to her face, Margaret could hardly breathe as she took that woman in.

"That's me?" She couldn't believe it and stepped closer, the edges of the dress pulling along the carpet of the dais. The woman in the mirrors came closer. "How can that be?"

"It's who you've always been," the beautiful younger man on the edge of the mirror answered.

Margaret began to laugh, swishing the skirt, practically spinning in place. "No wonder you can't keep your hands off me!" She laughed and laughed. Elias joined her, seizing her hand to gallantly spin her.

"My beautiful Margaret," he said. And for that moment, she believed him.

He spun her back into his embrace until she faced him, their breaths continuing the dance. She fell into his eyes, so blue and clear and penetrating, like he saw all her secrets. She knew she was going to kiss him. She smiled broadly at the thought, as she felt the draw of what was coming. Except, then, Elias's eyes flickered down, before double-taking to stare at her toothy smile, his eyebrows shooting up in surprise. Instinctively, her smile collapsed as she recognized that something was very wrong, but was unsure what.

"Margaret... can you open your mouth for me again?" he asked gently, his thumb teasing at her lower lip to encourage her to do so.

"Why?" she demanded, sharpness in her tone.

"Elias," another voice cut in. Both of them turned toward the double French doors to see Rosaleen standing there, her eyebrows furrowed together. "There is a dog here to see you."

That was when Margaret registered the sound of yapping that had been going on for a while. They all turned to see a small, white dog rush up past Rosaleen, skidding around her feet to bolt straight for Elias.

"It's okay, Rosaleen," Elias said, kneeling down as the dog approached. The dog perched its front paws on his leg and proceeded to yip and yowl, almost like it was attempting to speak.

"Slow down, Ally, take your time," Elias said to the little dog.

It huffed at him and continued its strange yowling. Margaret looked up at Rosaleen and her assistants, all three openly staring. What was happening here was weird.

Before she could say anything, like ask Elias if he had lost his flipping mind, he straightened up.

"I'm really sorry, Margaret. We're going to have to rain check."

"What is going on?" she hissed between her teeth.

"This outing simply seems cursed," he non-answered, then seized her hand, charging for the door. "Rosaleen, I am sorry, but we'll have to just take this one today. Please charge me for it. We can't wait, I have to go."

"Of course," Rosaleen replied, concerned, as she hustled out of the way so he could pass.

"Oh, and send the other clothing she wore into the store to my apartment at my expense!" he called over his shoulder.

"What's wrong, Elias?" Margaret managed to ask as they left the shop, her bare feet feeling strange on the stone smooth cobbles beneath her.

"My Lady is calling me," he answered as he led her down the tunnel a little further. They turned into an open doorway with a sign that had an image of a wood door above it. The door theme continued as other doors lined the small alley-shaped store. They were all the same type, cheap, white slabs of plywood with knobs of plain, clear crystal. A stocky woman held one of the doors open as a couple walked through into...well, it was hard for Margaret to see or understand what it was she was looking at. The door blocked her view, closing before she could puzzle it out.

The stocky woman turned to her newest customers, passing an eye over the dog, then the too-fancy dress, before shrugging. "Where to?"

Elias held out a hand and dropped a handful of small crystals into the stocky woman's waiting palm. "Two destinations."

"Do you have keys?" the stocky woman asked.

He smoothly pulled out two keys from his pocket. One was an old brass skeleton key and the other was a newer, cheap-looking key that one would open a storage locker with.

"Okay, easy enough then. Please step up to any door of your choosing, it doesn't matter which, they are all the same. Once I've inserted the key and initiated the door, you will have five minutes to step through, or you will have to pay for another Door Opening. Once you have stepped through and the door has shut, your key will appear in the lock on the other side. If there is no lock on the other side, the key will fall to the ground, at which time you may retrieve it. Thank you for choosing Door Openings Emporium for your fast travel needs," the stocky woman recited from rote, her tone the essence of boredom. "Which key first?"

"The brass one, please," Elias said, and she stuck it into one of the doors.

"Elias, what's happening?" Margaret asked as the door opened into...well, again, she couldn't suss out what she was looking at. It was all colors and no colors, all shapes and no shapes, like ghosts writhing over each other in a soup. A feeling of apprehension gripped her spine at the site. Margaret sure as hell had no intention of walking through.

"It's a door home. Don't worry, completely safe when opened by a professional Opener. I'll be home later. I promise, I'll make this up to you," he said as he unceremoniously pushed her through the door.

A sensation of cold and warmth swept over her and then a grayed-out version of Elias's apartment formed around her. After a moment, the colors bled back in. She found herself standing inside the front door, which shut on its own behind her. A second later, there was a clink as the brass key hit the ground. Then all was quiet.

CHAPTER 8

TWO DAYS WENT BY, AND ELIAS STILL HAD NOT COME BACK. AT FIRST, Margaret simply waited. Once she stripped off the beautiful starlight dress and hung it up, she climbed into jeans and a sweater and took up her spot at the counter on her stool. Grabbing the newspaper, she busied herself with that for most of the evening. When she became hungry, she pulled out cold bits from the fridge. She contemplated making some coffee and staying up to wait for him, but she dismissed that thought with a terse, "I'm not his mother," and instead went to have a shower. Then she went to bed, waking the next morning to a still-empty apartment.

She enjoyed the quiet for a little while, but she could only occupy herself for so long. Breakfast of toast and coffee was simple enough. She even made herself a second toast dressed with peanut butter and that strawberry syrup stuff since there was no jam. It was all right.

A fresh newspaper magically appeared on the counter. She read it end to end, some words came back to her in the exercise. Many more she passed over as unimportant if she couldn't remember them. She even attempted the crossword but abandoned it to complete the word search instead. All the while, Elias's key stared at her from where she had left it on the corner of the island counter. It taunted her as bad as the distant, ever-present sound of the crying baby.

Ignoring them both, she thought about watching TV, but instead got dressed.

As the day wore on, the crying baby grew louder, closer. Where was Elias? She realized that when she was with him, the ghostly sounds were absent. With him gone...

Back in the main room, she picked up the key that had returned with her the day before and examined it closer. It was literally a dark brass skeleton key with blocky, crooked teeth. Small crystals filled the eye sockets, instead of the typical empty space. As Margaret turned it in the light, a soft sheen of lavender reflected back at her. Even if she wanted to test it in a lock, just to see what would happen, there were no keyholes in the whole place that fit a key like that. Not knowing what else to do with it, she set the key back on the counter.

By the time she grew hungry, she realized there was scant other food in Elias's kitchen beyond toast. That problem solved itself an hour later. The doorbell rang just before a delivery kid let himself in with his own key, his earphones blaring so loud Margaret could almost make out the words. He dropped two boxes of food on the counter and walked out, popping his gum and never once making eye contact with her. He didn't even wait for a tip. Margaret heard the hum of the electric lock as he locked the door after himself, then all was quiet again. Shaking her head, she made herself some lunch then put the rest of the food away. As she did, she got it in her head that she probably remembered how to make cookies, only to discover she had mostly forgotten. She abandoned the kitchen in disgust, leaving a terrible mess in her wake. Elias could clean it when he got home.

Except, when he hadn't come home the next day, she made herself clean it up. It wasn't as thorough a job as he would have done, but it was cleaner. She wasn't a housekeeper.

She watched two hours of TV, never settling on anything.

Finally, she made herself go upstairs to Raymond's apartment. The number of books he had overwhelmed her, but she studied the map on the wall a little further. As she leaned in to read the tiny printed names leafing out from each pushpin, she wondered what this map was about. Finally, a book attracted her eye. A picture book from World War II. Post-its marked several pages. Each note had other titles and page numbers listed on them—which led her to the stack of books still on the table, which led her to other pages marked with post-it notes, which led to paragraphs highlighted in various gentle colors. As she read, a picture formed for her until she began to understand what the map was about. A young man, from the heart of Africa, traveled to war-torn Europe. A passage about a battle. A passage about the underground resistance. An incident. A tragedy. A triumph. Pawing through one man's journey, pulled from other people's research, hours later, Margaret realized these notes represented not just one lifetime's research but a second tangential lifetime wafting its way through the first.

"Elias," she whispered out loud as the realization dawned. She went to another shelf. More books, each with different colored post-its sticking out of their pages, but these books were about another time a hundred years prior. Then it made sense, as she investigated the next bookshelf full of books about the turn of the twentieth century.

"*Sistah,*" a voice called, making Margaret jump out of her skin with a small screech.

"Who the hell...?" she shouted, spinning around in place and seeing no one. Holding still as a mouse, she listened hard, but there was nothing. Setting down the book in her hands, she whipped open the door hard and stormed into the hallway.

"Who's there!?" she roared down the empty hallway. Only it wasn't empty. Stopping, she held herself still as she stared toward the far-left side door. The one door on that whole floor she hadn't explored yet. In front of it was and was not a man. There was no other way for her to describe it. Her eyes saw nothing standing in front of the door, and yet in her mind, she "saw" the figure of a familiar black man smiling at her. Then he stepped through the door.

She followed him, attacking the handle of the door like a raging cat. Barely noticing the change of air pressure as she did, her hand snaked in to the side, immediately finding the light switch, an overly large metal thing that clicked on hard.

Blinking, she stared at what should have been another mid-sized, corner apartment.

The room was huge.

Beyond the door, the space was easily as large as the ballroom downstairs. Wide as well as long, it should have cut into Raymond's apartment. Sconces hung every five feet along the walls. It felt like walking into a cave, her steps echoing slightly as she trod down a short flight of very wide stairs into the room. The stairs themselves were actually landings, but she barely noticed as she moved through the myriad of things all around her. On pedestals and inside glass containers rested historical objects. It was like entering a museum with everything perfectly preserved.

She stopped beside one case that held silver figurines of different sorts and one large lump of melted-together silver. Focusing on the strange lump for a moment, she recalled seeing something like it before, examples of slag created by the Chicago fire's intense heat, melting coins and such together.

Another case held very old weapons. Powder and shot pistols laid in a wood box lined with rubbed green velvet. Strangely enough, a bullet also rested in the space between the barrels of opposing weapons. Beside it sat a red wood drum, bound around its body with ropes. A proud eagle and shield had been painted on its front, with numbers written in Roman numerals decorating a painted banner over the eagle's head. Next to that was a leather sheath, holding the worn metal handle of a knife. Rudely carved into the surface of the sheath were the words: Wizard of Death.

Behind the case, solemnly hung three flags. One was an old, tattered United States flag, the stars ringed in a circle on the patch of faded blue. The middle-most was white with an embellished blue shield in the center and the words United States Army, Army of the Potomac, and Chicago, Illinois. The third flag was a French flag, with single strips of blue, white, and red sewn sloppily together as if made by someone with little true skill. In the center of the white band was the cross of Lorraine, the symbol of the French Resistance.

"Oh, Elias," Margaret said softly, tenderly touching the Resistance flag. "It's all true." She wasn't sure why at that moment, she truly believed it, but staring at that simple, tattered flag made his age seem more real. Turning toward the rest of the room, she spied a rack of clothes. She went to it and pulled out a few outfits. The older ones were wrapped in protective plastic. She even recognized some of the time periods the clothing had to have been from.

"Really? A zoot suit?" She laughed as she slid the blue pinstriped, straight-out-of-a-gangster-movie suit back on the rack. "You've liked fancy clothes your whole life, huh?"

She continued her exploration of the room, finding other treasures from around the world, another story of several lifetimes, carefully preserved. Putting together the story of the man she had chosen to stay with, she was particularly interested in the wall covered with photos, all framed, all ranging from the old daguerreotypes to the black-and-white film to the various stages of color. In the opposing corner hung paintings. Many of the images had versions of Elias in them somewhere, standing beside a myriad of different people. So many people he had loved and cared for, many of whom were now long gone.

For the first time in forever, Margaret felt so young.

After a few hours of careful exploration, hunger stopped her. It had been ages since she had felt so excited; it had obviously whetted her appetite. She went downstairs to the kitchen and fixed another bland, but easy-to-make meal for herself, only to realize as she sat down to eat how deeply tired she was. As she took herself to bed, she thought of Raymond's maps and the books he had been studying. If he had been tracing Elias's history before he died, he had to have known about the magical warehouse room beside his apartment. Had that been his great work? One that she could finish? To know Elias the way Raymond had been attempting. To complete something bigger than herself? The idea burned through her veins hotter than any drug she had ever taken. And with those thoughts, she fell asleep to true silence for the first time.

"*Sistah, wake up. He needs you now.*" The voice that cut through her sleep was warm and strongly accented. "*Sistah.*"

Sitting bolt upright in Elias's bed, Margaret about jumped out of her skin as she looked into the face of the young Raymond, standing patiently at the end of the bed.

"What.... what...?!" she tried to stutter out.

"He needs you, Sistah, hurry," Raymond said, pointing up with a finger as he looked toward the ceiling, then the ghost was simply gone.

Margaret could barely breathe. *What was happening? Who needed...?*

She knew the answer. Knew it deep in her bones. Glancing out the window, she saw the trees across the street violently bouncing as the night sky boiled with fast-moving clouds. The city's light pollution made them visible as they roiled.

Not knowing what else to do and driven by the unspecified urgency, Margaret found her jeans and sweatshirt and pulled them on as she hurried. She stopped short as her eyes fell on the starlight dress, waiting in the closet on its plain, wood hanger. The impulse to put it on overwhelmed her. That didn't make sense, though, why would she need to put on such a beautiful dress to go.... Well, she didn't know where she was going, but it certainly didn't require a fashion show.

Still....

Setting aside reason to follow instinct, Margaret quickly slipped into the dress, letting the slinky, satiny finish slide smoothly across her skin. Like it had before, the dress brought with it a feeling of beauty and ease. The skirt kissed the ground around her bare feet and everything about it felt perfect and right. The dress must have been blessed.

"Hurry, Sistah," Raymond's voice called from far, far away from no particular direction.

Heeding his call, she turned and left the bedroom to head to the hidden stairs leading up.

"No, Sistah. This way. He's on the roof," Raymond's voice echoed to her left. She turned to see the front door open. She had yet to explore past Elias's front door, but what little she saw when she came and went it had been unremarkable. Past his door was a short section of hallway that ended in a dead-end. Yet, that made little sense. There should have been more apartments taking up space on this floor. Coming to the three

blank walls, Margaret felt that same tingle of wrongness. She laid a curious hand against the unblemished surface. Her skin met cold metal instead of stucco wall. The illusion of a wall dissolved, revealing the gold-plate of the fabled elevator.

It binged open.

She stepped inside, her bare feet noting the coldness of the fake, stone-like tiles covering the floor. A short column of numbered buttons waited to be pushed beside the sliding door, which softly closed after she entered. The button at the top was labeled "R." She pushed it, deciding "R" for roof was logical enough.

A gentle *whir* accompanied the pulling sensation, underscored by a tiny tinkling bell for each floor. At the top, the door slid aside and wind filled the small compartment, like a mini-tornado. Immediately, Margaret's dress swirled around her, making her belatedly regret not putting on underwear. She had been in such a hurry, she hadn't even realized until she had to pull a Marilyn Monroe. How foolish she must have looked, an old woman in a too-fancy dress and no underwear. Where did she think she was? In a romance novel?

As quickly as it had come in, the wind danced out, taking Margaret's breath with it. She dared to look out of the elevator door, which began to close until she skittered out, triggering the safety feature to slide it open again.

His back to the elevator, Elias stood on the parapet wall, unheeding of the drop to the street below. The fierce wind whipped his long, loose hair and his unbuttoned shirt danced around him, accentuating the tension of his back muscles. Like Margaret, he stood barefoot, his fancy dark shoes lying on top of his coat, both abandoned on the roof near the elevator door.

Coldness seeped into Margaret as she stood on the partially frozen roof staring at Elias as he raised his hands to the boiling sky.

"Are you crazy?!" Margaret shouted over the wind as it billowed her skirts again.

"Glorious!" Elias shouted as he spun on his feet.

For a heart-wrenching minute, Margaret thought he was going to go over the edge, or someone would hear him shouting and call the police, but his body stayed put, not losing its balance in the slightest. He threw back his head and laughed maniacally.

Just great! He's gone nuts. She had dealt with crazy before. Most people living on the streets were crazy or working their way there one trauma at a time.

"What are you talking about, Margaret? He's been nuts this entire time," she grumbled to herself as she crossed the roof to pull his ass back to safety.

"Where the hell have you been? Do you know how long I've been waiting for you?" She continued to berate him as she approached, cutting off his cawing.

"My Lady called me, and I went," he answered. Elias gestured fiercely with his hands toward the sky again and the wind billowed up, lifting him a few feet straight up into the air. Graceful as a dancer, he landed back on the edge of the building.

"Who the hell is this Lady you keep talking about?" Margaret redirected her steps urgently to his new position, moving slower than she should have against the buffets of the wind.

"She is my only purpose."

That stung more than it should. "And what the fuck am I then?"

"A wonder to behold!" He made a fist and the wind stopped, leaving the world an eerie, dead calm.

"Are you controlling the wind?" Margaret asked, her voice echoing loudly in the new silence.

"My first Talent." He made a fist again, popping it open to show a tiny cyclone whirling in the palm of his hand, barely visible as it had very little dust or detritus lending form to its body. "Are you proud of me, Uncle? See what I can do?" he shouted at the sky.

"Elias, please come down," she started to say, finally reaching his side.

"Spirits that rise, come see me fly!" he shouted again. The wind spun around him then it spun *him* around, lifting him up in the air like a deranged god. He stared down at her from above, floating. The light pollution below lit him up, making his form a dark shadow against its diffused, yellowed glow. Far off in the distance, Lake Michigan boiled and roiled in tempo with the sky.

"Elias!" Margaret shouted again.

Finally, he looked down, directly at her, and stopped. He seemed struck by what he saw and it calmed the wind. The storm paused for a moment, still roiling in the sky, but almost like it waited for something.

Slowly, he floated back down to hover in front of her. "My beautiful Margaret," he whispered. She felt his gaze rove down her body, the dress clinging to her form in the wind, the metallic bits winking in the scant light. Her face warmed, battling between shyness and excitement at his gaze. Yet, she felt right and even a little proud of how she looked in the dress, even if it was ridiculous to wear it on a rooftop during a storm. She liked the expression on his face when he looked at her in it. As his feet touched the ground, she could see his hard, manic, hungry eyes, despite the shadow across his face. His hand crept down his chest as his eyes drank her in, the motion both sensual and drunken. For a moment, Margaret almost believed his hand actually caressed her. It was disturbing.

"What the hell is wrong with you?" she cried out, startled.

He laughed again. His eyes were completely blue. Not his normal shade of dark blue. Instead, they were the color of a robin's egg. No iris, no pupil, just a solid, milky blue.

"Oh, I am probably spell-cursed," he said. "Things went a little..." he paused as he reconsidered his words, "out of hand." He spun in a circle around Margaret in an impossibly smooth and too fast motion for him to be moving with his feet.

"What do you mean by...?" She didn't get the rest out before he continued.

"Everything was mostly fine, of course. My Lady had sorted much of it out before I got there. Truly, I think Ally was over-reacting. But teenagers are like that. You're pretty." He looked up at the sky, distracted.

"You mean the dog? Over-reacting? You were gone for two days! And now you say you're...spell cursed or whatever!"

"I said you're pretty, Margaret," he repeated.

"I heard you. You're deflecting again."

He growled in his throat, furrowing his eyebrows at her. "I don't want to talk about it, but I will if you keep pushing. I'd rather take you dancing in that dress." His hand whipped out to capture her hand, but she yanked it free.

"Well, too bad. I am going to push it. What happened?"

"I got spell-cursed!" he shouted at her, chewing each word in frustration.

"What is that?"

He turned his fingers toward himself like he intended to claw out whatever was inside him. "My Love...There is too much magic in here," he said, digging his fingers into his own chest. "I burn with it. I pulled it into myself and the spell turned against me."

"You sound really bad...do we need to take you to a hospital? What do we do here? Elias?"

He cocked his head at her. "You're worried about me?"

"Of course I am!"

He regarded her a minute longer, giving her a smile that was both happy and sad, which was alien with his opaque eyes. "It's fine. You don't need to worry about me. I'm not human. But you know that, don't you?" His tone held a distinct note of threat as he pronounced those words.

Margaret swallowed. She realized she was probably in danger, but what else could she do? Run? From a being like him? In that moment, she realized she no longer sought her death. She saw herself as living and the idea that *he* would do her harm...it was ludicrous. She trusted him, but right now he was lost in darkness.

She understood darkness.

"I know, Elias."

He pinched his eyebrows together. "What do you mean, you know?"

"You're an angel, Elias. I know." When he didn't respond to that, she stumbled on. Now that the truth was out there, she might as well say it all. "I know you wanted me to believe that story about your son and such, but I know it's a lie. But it's okay. It's your cover, right? So you can dwell undetected amongst us."

When he laughed, Margaret began to falter.

She continued, "You came to save... me..."

"Margaret. I'm no angel. I'm the Wizard of Death!"

She swallowed. "But just now, you were flying!"

"It's wind magic. I am a very good Wind Mage. Among other things."

"Talents are just people. I don't know much, but I know that. They don't live forever! They don't stay young forever!"

"But I can, potentially. We are Magi." He stated it like it answered something, like she should know what he meant, but Margaret had no idea what the question was.

"Elias, you're scaring me," she challenged.

"This is part of the deal, isn't it? Accepting what we learn about each other? It's what I agreed to." His voice was low, talking more to himself than her.

Shifting his stance, he thrust his hand out to Margaret, palm open in offer. "Come with me to Neverland!" he crowed. The wind gathered again, launching them into the air. Not knowing what else to do, she threw her arms around Elias's neck. He gripped her back.

As the world spun away from them, Margaret tried not to cry out, burrowing her mouth against Elias's shoulder to suppress the high-pitch scream rising involuntarily from her throat. Below, too far below, was nothing but streaks of moving light and rough shapes. Then the wind's speed increased, and she felt her body being pulled away from Elias's as they spun in the air. She tightened her grip on his shoulders as they peeled apart, but it did no good. The wind had its own plans. Higher and higher they went, plunging into the clouds and then above into the clear, starlit sky. Margaret couldn't even cry out anymore, it was too much like a dream.

At last, their ascent began to slow. As it did, Elias let go so his hands slid down her arms until they gripped her hands. "No, don't!" Margaret cried, but he squeezed them tight, his eerie, creamy blue eyes grinning.

"Let me fly with you just once, Margaret," he said, sounding mostly normal for a moment. They continued to spin, but the wind seemed calmer. The stars above spread out across the sky. It was breathtaking. As the spinning slowed, Margaret felt more able to move. Elias let go of one of her hands and she was able to turn out to get the panoramic view.

"We're not falling," she realized.

"I won't let you fall," he answered and she believed him. She let go of his other hand and she felt the air around her holding her up like she floated in water. Moving was a simple matter, pushing against the force of the wind, and after a few tries, she had the trick of it. Continuing the water idea, it was almost like swimming. She even began to laugh at the freedom of movement.

"We're dancing among the stars!" she cried out, the skirt of her dress billowing around her.

"We're high enough up that we're on the edge of the earth's gravity," he called.

That made her pause as a scrap of knowledge pushed its way through her brain's cobwebs. "But how can we still breathe?"

He gestured gracefully again and a warm breeze danced over her skin, making her tingle as strongly as if he had caressed her with a hand. "I am bringing us air and warmth. Normally, we would have frozen to death by now, even if it wasn't autumn. You may not know this, but I am very skilled."

She caught his hand as he pirouetted about her, continuing their dance. Swirling into his arms, she captured his cheek in a hand and kissed him. He returned it, and she giggled in delight. If this was a dream, may she never wake up. She could die now. How could she live after this? Except, now she wanted to live. She genuinely, deeply wanted it.

Coaxing his fingers through her newly cut hair, she shivered. She wanted more as she skated over a cloud, disturbing its serene puffiness, brushing the cooler air with her foot.

"You are so beautiful," he whispered, catching her up as she laughed from a spin. Gently, he touched her lips once more with his own before laying his forehead against hers. "And I'm going to destroy that. I'm sorry, Margaret."

By the time she comprehended what he said, it was too late. Nothing violent happened, but the experience was intense. Some distant part of her felt his forehead pressing against hers, yet it was drowned out by the sensations of hot and cold lacing through her body, stretching inside her like roots of a tree through earth. She would swear she saw light, though her eyelids remained closed. If anyone looked up at that moment, would the two of them simply look like lightning in the clouds, only lasting entirely too long?

As the sensations began to fade, Margaret took a deep all-the-way-to-her-toes breath. Elias cupped her face as he lifted his forehead from hers so she could inhale freely.

"What did you do? What happened?" she gasped out loud.

"I was right," he answered, his expression once more both happy and sad. "What I feared was true is true. This proves it."

"Elias! Will you get to the point! Tell me what you mean!" Margaret cried out. Then, she blinked twice. "Your eyes?" she questioned again, reaching fingertips toward them.

"They're normal again, aren't they?" he concluded. She nodded as she stared deeply into their ocean blue depths.

He pressed her fingertips against his cheek. "Margaret, look at your hands," he whispered.

She did. She recognized them.

So often, when she looked down at her fingers, she saw the thin, papery skin and blue veins, crisscrossed with scars; the hands of a stranger. The hands she saw now were *her* hands. The skin smooth and filled, its surface free of any signs of age, her nails pink with health. Turning them over, she stared at her palms as if the answers were written there.

"I don't...I don't understand."

Her examination went up her arms, down her body, moving the dress aside to see her legs, now strong and beautifully long, her skin firm and full of living color.

As she stretched and strained in her new self-discovery, her spine and joints popped and crackled, sliding everything that had been out of alignment for years back into place all at once.

"Oh, geez!" she exclaimed. "Elias, what's happening?" That was when she heard her own voice, no longer deeper and crackling, but airier and almost musical.

"There are only two practical ways to resolve a spell curse. One is to burn out the energy with a great expenditure of power, the other..." he chuffed a laugh, "kill two birds with one stone. You can pass the energy over to another Magi."

"You healed me? I'm young again?"

He hesitated.

"Elias!" Margaret commanded, and he flinched.

"You healed yourself. You've been healing yourself for weeks. When you took the magic that fed the curse inside me, your body had enough power to restore itself fully. Instinctively."

"So, now I'm cursed?!" Margaret asked, alarmed.

"No, not at all." He gathered her close, hugging her with his whole body to reassure her. "Without the magic to feed it, the curse dissolved, unable to hold together. It was a hex to inebriate me, or rather my Lady, but I took it from her."

"Why didn't your *Lady* help you, then?" Margaret demanded, not thinking much of this lady if she would let such a terrible thing happen to Elias.

"I'm pretty sure I just flew off at that point. I need to let her know that I'm alright and make sure she is well." He kissed Margaret's cheek softly. "Thank you."

"For what? I don't understand... what did I do?"

"You are a Magi, like me," he pronounced. "I hadn't meant to tell you this way, but it's probably best that you see for yourself. You are the kind of woman who needs proof."

"What? I don't understand. I'm not like you..." She retreated a little from him, just in time to notice that they had begun descending toward the earth again. Wisps of clouds pushed past them as they came closer to the main cloud, the storm roiling afresh. Margaret felt the electricity building in the air and for a moment she panicked, fearing she was about to be struck.

"Hold on to me!" Elias grabbed her and they plummeted straight down into the cloud. *What good is it running away from lightning?* Margaret wondered as they fell through the sky. But then there was a loud flash and a bright boom as the charge arched, instead, through the clouds, outlining the dark shape of a jet plane trying to descend through the storm.

Together, she and Elias plummeted to earth until they had cleared the cloud. More air burst up to meet them, and they slowed. Margaret almost didn't trust it when her feet touched the roof of Elias's building. She remained clutched in Elias's arms for several breaths, until her heart calmed down enough to get out of her ears.

"Margaret, are you alright?" Elias asked, gently stroking her hair as she clung to him.

"I'm alive," she whispered, then the truth came out louder. "I'm alive. I'm going to live! I'm alive! And young!" Her excitement burst forth as she began to jump, gripping his arms into a new kind of leaping dance as she spun him around, laughing. "Oh my god, I am alive! Look at me! Look at me, Elias! Look at these hands, my face! This means..." Her bouncing stopped as a new piece fell into place. "I can start over? Right? Is that right? I can have another chance?"

"Yes, beloved one, it means you can start over from the beginning. Your body will continue to heal until you're at the epitome of your adult-self in terms of health. As long as you don't use your magic, the magic will maintain you that way."

"I have magic?" She raised her hands again. "This is magic?"

"Yes," he nodded, his wind-blown hair sweeping forward. She caught a strand and stared at it, before turning him to better catch the light from the street below. He allowed her to shift him. A swath of silver now cut through the dark strands. She turned his face into the light and ran a finger along the corner of his right eye where crow's feet now dented his skin. He looked like a man in his fifties. Still beautiful, but definitely more mature. "As you use your magic...or rather, the more of it you use, the less there will be for your life force to feed itself. It makes little difference usually and always regenerates with time and rest, but you can go too far, expend too much. When this happens, you will age and break your body down."

"Then, the drugs..." Another piece landed in place.

"Yes, you would have discovered this much sooner if you hadn't harmed your body with drugs and diseases. Years ago, in fact. You probably would have noticed that you remained youthful as those around you aged," Elias said.

"This is why I'm still alive? After all this time. My...*my magic* kept me alive."

"Yes," he agreed.

She sobered suddenly. She could hear it, off in the distance. The crying.

"Why didn't it save my baby?"

Elias closed his eyes slowly before forcing them open again.

"Because we can still be killed. Most diseases won't affect us, or at least not for very long. Our magically enhanced immune systems fight them. Most wounds and damage done to us heals relatively quickly." Then he raised his right hand, shaping it into a gun, the tip pointing straight into Margaret's head. "But if someone gets us too fast, hurts us too greatly, ends our life before our magic can stabilize us..." He fired the symbolic gun and dropped his hand to his side. Margaret instinctively rocked back in response to his gesture. "I'm not a doctor or a healer of any particular skill, but my guess is your body miscarried the baby before it could stabilize itself."

Margaret pressed her hand against her abdomen, the flesh firm again under the fine material of the dress, the paunch her baby had left her completely gone. "They said I would never have children again."

"They were wrong. Your body will fully restore itself, if it hasn't already. You can have as many children as you want."

A tear, hot and furious, spilled from Margaret's eye, shooting down her face as she crumpled under her grief. She looked up at Elias and reached out a pleading hand. He was there, holding her again. "All those years. *All* those years," she repeated as he rocked her. After a few moments, she was able to straighten, her voice returning to her.

"So, you lied. You're not immortal. I'm not immortal," she said, with no judgment.

"Not lied. Oversimplified," he shifted. "I find it difficult to explain...myself to others."

She chuckled. "I noticed." She managed to take a full, deep breath.

His hand still rested at her waist. Stable, strong. He anchored her as her mind whirlwinded, trying to assimilate the new knowledge it now had.

"Now what?" she muttered.

"What do you want to do?" he asked softly. His voice, tender and warm, sent shivers down her spine like it had so many times before, but this time it was different. Because she was different.

"I want you," she said. Her heart trilled as she wrapped her arms around his neck and kissed him full on the mouth. Only this time, she had no intention of stopping there. He hesitated for just a moment before sinking a hand in her hair. She felt the fire burning between them and her body's ache in response. It was time. Time, at last, to take what she had wanted for so long. While his other hand set in her hair, the one at her waist slipped down further. Urging that hand on, Margaret raised her leg to curl around his body. The elegant star-filled dress cupped her full hip, forcing his hand to move faster and find new purchase down her thigh, coming to rest under her knee.

Everything sang within her. This was what she wanted. What she needed now more than anything. Her reaffirmation of life. To share what was inside her with him. She was alive, impossibly young again, and in the arms of a beautiful man who she...loved?

A tightness gripped her heart as the feeling inside it stressed outward, then burst forth and ignited her body with joy. Love. Yes. She felt love. The love she had sought and been denied so many years ago. The love she could now have ...

"Margaret, stop!" Elias growled as he pulled her head away, his hands releasing their tangled hold.

Her own hands still floated in the air after him as he took several steps away, running his shaking hands through his hair, followed by the telltale yank on his ear. The colder air of the fall-winter mix in the storm knifed through the bubble of warmth they had been in.

"What's wrong?" she asked, her voice sounding small and frightened. A thrum of warning came from within as she realized too late what had happened. She was vulnerable. She had taken a risk exposing herself like that. Already the hammer inside was falling to smash her elation as she recognized the look on his face.

"Margaret, I'm sorry. I...I can't."

"No, don't do this, Elias..." she squeaked out as she wrapped her arms around her middle. Why was this happening again?

"No, please, Margaret. You have to understand. Now that we know..."

"Elias..." she pleaded.

"I can't do this with you anymore... I told you..."

She barely heard the words as she ran toward the doorway. She didn't want to hear what else he had to say. She had heard it all before. There was a pause for a moment when she realized the door opened onto a stairwell and not the elevator, but it was barely a heartbeat before she had plummeted halfway down them. She heard him calling after her.

"Margaret! Wait!" Elias shouted from behind her, but she didn't. "You have your whole life ahead of you now! You can be anything you want, have anyone...You're starting your life over, I just can't...do that with you! Please understand."

She barreled out the door at the bottom of the stairs and swung around to the next set, barely seeing the hallway where Raymond's apartment was. She hauled open the bookcase door and pounded down those steps, her bare feet hardly noticing the stab of the metal treads as she went.

She didn't stop until she reached his apartment, passed through to his bedroom, and slammed the door shut behind her. Her numbed fingers managed to lock it.

"Margaret, you need to understand," he continued, on the other side of the door. She covered her face with her hands, hardly able to bear hearing his voice. "We agreed, remember? This wasn't going to be forever. I'm not looking for forever. It's not personal. And it's not fair. It's not fair to you when you've got a second chance at a full life. Margaret?"

She noticed her reflection in the mirror over his bed. The beautiful young woman, staring up at her through her fingers, dressed in a beautiful gown of starlight, her dark hair elegantly cut short. The woman in the mirror picked up a vase near the door she leaned against and flung it at the glass, smashing it into a million glorious pieces.

"Margaret!" Elias banged frantically at the door. She ignored him. Instead, she proceeded into the bathroom and murdered that mirror as well. She wanted to find a third mirror to destroy, but there simply wasn't one.

She was too numb in spirit to notice the glass cutting her feet as she moved into the closet and tore off the dress. It was more awkward than she expected. The dress was very well made, but her struggles were worth it once she was free. She flung the torn remains to the floor of the closet and redressed herself in jeans and a grey sweater. She found her coat, as well as his gloves and a hat. She indulged in two pairs of socks inside the shoes, the bleeding having stopped well before she even noticed the wounds.

Opening the door to the bedroom, she exited to find Elias sitting at the kitchen island, staring at the floor. He was still barefoot, but he had re-buttoned his shirt. He rose once he laid eyes on her.

"You said you would give me money," she said flatly.

He said nothing, and she met his eyes, keeping hers hard and straight on to hide her pain. She saw in his expression, all the things he wanted to say, all the arguments he wanted to make. She watched him read all the things she would say in response. Finally, he nodded, not a word exchanged between them, and led the way down into his shop. There he went into a safe under the counter and opened it without unlocking it. Except he had, she could feel it now, clearer than before, the off-ness releasing around the safe. Now she understood what that wrongness meant.

He pulled out a large packet of bills, wrapped in a band with the number $10,000 printed on it. Setting it on the counter, he closed the safe. "If you can wait, I can get you more."

"This is fine," she said and pocketed the bundle without further preamble. She turned to move toward the front door.

"You don't have to leave, Margaret," he said as she approached it. "I will help you get started. You don't have to do this alone."

"What's the point of a new life if it's just going to be the same shit anyway?" She unlocked the door and left without a further backward glance.

CHAPTER 9

THE BUILDING SMELLED OF HUMANNESS AND SICKNESS. NO LIGHTS were on, only a gray glow filtering in through windows that had very little glass remaining. Someone at some time had made a paltry effort to cover a few windows with cardboard and even less effort to fix it again when it fell down. Cold air cut through the halls, but it didn't stop the writhing bodies inside from staying. While all of the buildings in the little fenced-in slice of city land were intended to be for affordable, low-income housing subsidized by the city of Chicago, the managers entrusted with them were so corrupt that many of the buildings had remained empty and unused and unmaintained. All the while, the managerial company collected their paycheck from the joke of the government. It didn't mean the buildings didn't sometimes have occupants. Often they did, but no one was collected rent. No one dared.

Margaret moved through the place, as familiar as if she were going home. There was no bittersweet nostalgia as she moved through the long, narrow hallway. She simply had nowhere else she could think of to go.

She passed a few people in the hallways and many more lying out in the individual "apartments." The doors had long since been burned for heat, so no concept of privacy remained. It didn't stop fornicators of all sorts going at it for a disinterested or overly interested audience. Most here were high on the latest street drugs. From what Margaret could tell, it was an old favorite repackaged, Devil's Sulphur, or D-phur, magic-infused to make it last longer, or stop your heart.

Margaret passed by a man smoking a plain cigarette in the hallway, the first person to give her a look up and down since she had entered. He pulled the homemade roll from his mouth, his words forming in the smoke. "Whoever you lookin' for isn't someone worth saving."

She pushed past him.

Somewhere someone coughed painfully. Somewhere someone laughed manically. None of these things bothered her a mere few weeks ago when she had been a no one. Had it really only been a few weeks?

It didn't matter. It wouldn't matter at all very soon.

The darkness came to greet her once she reached the Inner Sanctum on the second floor. As she hesitated at the threshold, a sick, miasmic smell wafted over her, mixed with some poor attempt to cover it with sandalwood and patchouli.

The room, at one time, had actually been two different apartments, but someone at some time had smashed through the wall between them, creating one long space. Lined up along the opposing walls were two rows of mattresses, bare, stained, and mostly full. At the far end were two wicker chairs that should have been on someone's back porch and probably had been at one time. Stolen and frayed, one was empty, and the other contained a man. He was rail-thin with long greasy hair and a just as long scraggly beard that was unkempt. He was dressed in old clothing that had darkened and stiffened with a patina of living. Looking up as she approached, he scratched hard at an angry patch of skin on his neck. He eyed her face, then her coat, obviously assessing its and her worth at the same time.

"I don't know anything," he finally said, looking away as if that would make her disappear.

"That's obvious," she snapped back.

It returned his attention to her. "What did you say to me, bitch?"

She ignored the threat in his voice and pulled out a twenty-dollar bill from her pocket, thrusting it at him. He stared at it, deciding. The bill was cleaner than most he saw in this place, but he took it just the same. She wouldn't have been the first moneyed person to come looking for their ruin. Without saying anything more, he nodded at the empty wicker chair and got to his feet, his long wiry body bowing exaggeratedly at the joints like it barely remembered how to function. An old coffee table, propped up on a paint can and cinderblock where its fourth leg should have been, stood between the chairs. Margaret skirted around it to sit down.

She had been in this room hundreds of times. She preferred the third mattress on the right, under the covered window. Not far away she saw a face she sort of recognized: an old man she had gone to the nearby soup kitchen to get some food with, so they wouldn't have to eat alone. As she sat there, she realized she had no idea what his name was. Of course, calling out to him was probably pointless anyway. His eyes probably wouldn't even register if he saw her.

Taking in all the bodies in the room, she asked herself what she was doing here, before shaking her head angrily, as if that would scatter thought away like sand.

"I know exactly what I'm doing here," she muttered out loud.

"Of course you do," the thin man said as he returned, setting a box down on the coffee table. His voice was stronger, darker. Then he asked in his thin, reedy voice, "You smoking it or injecting it?"

She stared at him a moment, a trembling skittering in her bones. What was she doing here?

"Injecting."

"Do you have your own needle?"

She blinked. That was a new question. "No."

He screwed his face up a second, not liking that answer.

"What's the problem?" she pressed.

"It's just...you obviously belong to someone, and the last thing I need is trouble..."

"I don't belong to anyone," she snapped.

The thin, reedy man smiled, showing rotted and missing teeth in equal measure. "Wrong. You belong to me," he said, a shadow with no source passed over his face.

She nodded. It was true. "You tried to tell me," she answered.

"You're so stupid." He turned back to the box, popping it open to pull out a thick, half-burned candle. He lit it with a cheap lighter, the flame looking like it burned too close to his skin, but he didn't seem to notice. A bent spoon joined the candle. Then he disappeared from the room once more, leaving her to stew. She jittered her leg, her feet itching to leave. No. She was just jittering for the fix. That was it. It had been so long. She needed it to make everything better, to set things the way they were before and should have stayed.

In the distance, she heard the baby crying, the darkness in the room amplified it, making it echo and thrum. *Come to me*, the baby's cry said to her. *Why don't you come? Why don't you pick me up? Why am I alone? I need you.*

"I'm coming, baby," she whispered, "I'll be with you soon." She planned to take enough of the stuff to blast herself into permanent oblivion. Finally end it all in one dosed finale. But something was different this time. Usually, when she heard the baby cry, anger, fear, regret, sheer physical pain would cut through her, as fresh as it was the day she had killed...she'd *lost* her baby. But now, all she saw in her mind's eye was herself holding her younger self, mothering and being mothered. It was a false memory. She knew that. Yet, she felt it still, the warmth in her chest, the relief of being allowed to be sad. Being told, "It wasn't your fault" and believing it. At least, *wanting* to believe that maybe that was true.

The thin, reedy man returned and tore open a plastic and waxed paper sleeve. The package looked like something stolen from a medical facility, being it was properly sealed and covered with small instructional type. "It's your lucky day," he said, rather proudly, before setting down the new needle next to the candle on top of its paper.

From one of the beds, a figure rose. It shambled over to the other side of the table, swaying and staring as the thin, reedy man poured some thick blood-like liquid onto the spoon from a repurposed cold medicine bottle, then sprinkled black powder generously on top. It immediately began to smoke and hiss, refreshing the prevalent, sulfurous smell in the room. He held it over the flame. After a minute, it began to boil, the black powder melting as it chemically bonded with the red liquid. Tiny droplets crept over the edge, curling around the bowl of the spoon.

Once the thin, reedy man was satisfied it was ready, he removed it from the flame. As he picked up the needle, the other encroaching junkie reached out to snatch it up.

"What the fuck are you doing, man?!" The thin, reedy man swiped up, splattering the liquid and knocking the junkie's hand away as he screeched. Those in the room still able stirred to look in the direction of the ruckus. The junkie stumbled back, easily thrown off balance. He curled sideways in a weak defensive pose like he expected to receive a beating. Instead, the darkness intensified in the room.

"You wasted my gifts," the darkness declared through the thin, reedy man. It was the greatest sin that could be committed in that place. Maybe the only sin. "You dare steal from me?"

"I thought it was for me!" the junkie whined.

"Nothing is yours. Not even your life. You are worthless."

"I am worthless," the junkie repeated.

"You belong to me." The darkness left the reedy man, lifting off him like a sentient shadow to move toward the junkie, who stumbled over another body, which gave a pitiful yelp but didn't move or otherwise notice the intrusion.

Margaret had seen this before. Everyone in the room had. No one moved to help the junkie as he whimpered in terror. Swiping uselessly at the unfeeling dark as it took him, he sank into the floor in a pool of black without even a cry for help. Not that any would have been given. Before he was completely consumed, the junkie went still as a corpse, no longer fighting as the darkness boiled over him like bubbling lava. Then it was gone. All that remained was a newly blackened smudge on the cheap wooden floor, one amongst uncountable others.

The thin, reedy man didn't watch what happened to the junkie; he shook his free hand, dripping everywhere with the red liquid that had spilled and burned. Despite the angry scores the liquid left on his hand, he seemed more annoyed than in pain.

"Wait here," he snapped, walking off with the spoon and needle in his unburned hand. The rest of the room settled back into their own personal oblivion.

The darkness continued to linger at Margaret's feet.

"This is bullshit," she muttered and pushed herself out of the chair, though she didn't really have an idea what she to do after that.

That's when another man appeared at the far doorway, and she dropped back into the chair.

He was tall, dressed in a long, dark trench coat and fedora, like he had just stepped out of some film Noir. He strolled confidently into the room, looking down at the forms along each wall, examining them in turn. Another one of the junkies, one of the few who had not rolled back over into oblivion, didn't seem to like the new stranger.

"Hey, what the hell do you think you're doing here?" the junkie spat, pushing himself up to his feet, leaving a stick-thin woman he had been holding on the mattress.

The new man turned to the latest junkie with an easy smile, looking him up and down, assessing. Probably accurately. Sometimes mafia types wandered in here to throw their weight around, making trouble or deals in equal measure. This guy definitely carried himself with the confidence of a man who knew he was dangerous and knew it was sexy.

"I'm looking for a woman named Margaret," he said and Margaret's heart stopped for a second.

Every instinct told her to jump up and run, but she didn't obey. She was stuck in the chair, realizing the darkness held her there, passively, but firmly.

If you run, he'll chase you. He'll catch you too. I'll keep you safe, the darkness purred, so softly only she could hear.

"I don't know no Margaret," the junkie answered, getting visibly angry at the intruder. "Now get the hell out of here."

The junkie took a swing, and predictably, the suave mafia guy stepped back to avoid it before grabbing the man by the back of his shirt and flinging him in the direction he was already pointed, slamming his face into the crumbling wall.

"What the hell is going on here?" the thin, reedy man demanded as he returned. "I don't need any more shit today."

The mafia man turned toward the newcomer, completely unperturbed by the junkie moaning uselessly behind him.

"Hello, I am looking for someone. I'm wondering if you can help me." Mafia man smiled.

"No. Now, get the hell out," the reedy man ordered, pointing at the door.

"Hmm, pity," the mafia man said, just as someone else entered the room.

"St. Benedict, did you find her?" the young woman called from the door, her nose wrinkling up at the smell. She had a curvy figure some magazines would call plus-size, dressed in a short leather jacket hanging open despite the cold. She wore a belt strapped to her waist, covered in pockets.

"I think so," he said, meeting Margaret's eyes when she flicked them toward him, giving her a satisfied cat-eating-the-canary smile. He opened the palm of his hand and rolled his fingers. Light appeared above the surface, forming a hologram of her old face. Now *that* was amazing. "Yeah, 'I think so' is the best I can say," he concluded, looking through the hologram at her.

The young woman followed his eyes, a wash of relief washing over her face. Why should she be relieved to see her? Margaret had never seen this woman in her life. Then, the new woman turned and shouted down the hallway, "Elias! She's in here."

Margaret's heart began to beat rapidly. He was here. *Elias* was here? Why?

"Who the fuck are you?" Margaret challenged. The woman stepped into the room to stand next to the one she called St. Benedict.

"My name's Rune Leveau, this is St. Benedict. I'm Elias's cousin."

"*You're* his cousin." Margaret eyed her up and down. She remembered him mentioning her. The owner of the bar. This was his only reason for living? His only family left in the entire world? Was she like him? A...Magi? Looking at the woman, she looked pretty young. Margaret passively wondered how old that pretty face really was.

"Yes, we've been looking for you. We're helping him find you."

"I said get the fuck out of here!" the thin, reedy man roared, pointing again to the exit.

"Margaret, come with us," Rune continued, flinching at, but ignoring the yelling. Her companion did not. Deliberately, he stepped around her, moving even closer to the front, never breaking eyes with the thin, reedy man. When he was close enough, he extended his hand to Margaret.

"If you want to come with us, come now," he said, "No one will stop you. I promise."

"I don't want to be saved," Margaret snapped, staring at his open hand.

"No one would stop her anyway," the darkness said, as it reasserted its control on the thin, reedy man. "They are all welcome to come, and they are all welcome to leave, as they wish." He returned to his task of remaking the syringe. More of the sickly smoke billowed around him, framing his features like a demon's horns. Gently, he tapped the side of the syringe, as if he was knocking out air bubbles. It was all for show. "Are you ready for this, my Margaret?

"Get it over with already," she growled harshly.

The demon smirked at the duo, who both glared back.

"Margaret, don't..." Rune started to say. Then Elias walked into the room.

He looked different again. More tired, less put together. He was dressed as he often was, in tight-fitting clothes, but this time just jeans and a hooded sweatshirt like anyone would have found in a second-hand shop, not the suave high-end stuff he usually wore. Unheeding of any of the tension in the room, he crossed straight to her as soon as his eyes landed on her.

His expression was so intense, she thought for a brief moment that he was going to hit her or yell at her, but all he did was drop to his knees before her, laying both hands on her knees like a supplicant.

"There you are, I found you," he breathed and leaned forward to press his forehead against those same knees a moment. "Are you alright?"

She wanted to shift away or push him off, as he desperately tried to get her to look at him. "I...I'm fine...Elias."

"I'm so sorry," he whispered.

"I don't care," she lied, pushing him away so she could stand, thrusting her arm out to the thin, reedy man. The demon within him smiled with delighted eyes and handed her the needle.

"Margaret, please, wait," Elias begged, but she refused to acknowledge him, her vision filled, instead, with the syringe, the dark red liquid inside promising peace from pain. From the memories. From the ghosts. "Come home with me. I want you to come back."

She let her actions be her retort.

Injecting it was easy, as practiced as she was, but she regretted it the minute the needle passed through her skin. Her body had healed too much and had forgotten the sensation of liquid fire as it tore through her veins like a wild flame on a dry hillside. Soon her senses dulled, warping away from the drab world. It was the same room as before, but now she saw the walls were made of fire. The others on the mattresses slept peacefully, their souls at peace. She could barely see them or the shadow figures speaking wordlessly. She could barely feel the pressure of Elias holding her from behind as the weight of her body gave way while her soul lifted away from it.

"Finally, some quiet," the demon said, more visible now that she had used his key and entered through his door. He stepped apart from the thin, reedy man, the darkness trailing behind him like a wafting cloak, corrupting everything it touched. The demon was real and solid as he came forward to cup her chin with one overly long, bony finger. "Do not worry, my little bitch, I will keep you good and under this time. You lasted so long before, but now..." he hissed in a breath and released a euphoric shudder, "what a gift to have you reset for another lifetime."

Fear slid through Margaret's heart as she realized what he meant. Before, with her life almost spent, her suffering would have been almost over. Except, her magic had kept it going, the very magic this beast consumed.

Leaning forward, his long tongue licked the side of her face and with it a long saliva-like string of light danced away from her. "Delicious."

She didn't care, she told herself. "I don't care."

The demon smirked and took up her hand to lead her back to the wicker chair, now a blackened throne of twisted, charred wood. She sat upon it obediently. This was where she belonged; this was what she deserved.

"This *is* what you deserve," the demon agreed out loud, before moving off to leave her in her numbing oblivion. Usually, her mind would go quiet with the drug's effect. Margaret would simply stay in the place of exhaustion, truly resting here in a way life would never let her. Usually. Except, today she felt... she felt? She should feel nothing. Something still connected her to the world she always wanted to leave behind.

She *felt* sad. She *felt* regret. She *felt* loved.

In response, the memory played, first as a thought, then it was really there. A woman, herself, wrapped her arms around her current self, warm and whispered, "I understand," over and over again, rocking her gently.

Tears burst forth from Margaret's eyes.

It was already too late. She had made the same choice again and this time there was no going back. Elias had come and offered to take her out of this place. Why hadn't she simply said yes? Why? She had done it once before. She could have said yes again, couldn't she?

"No, you needed to know for sure," her older self said, "I understand."

"But I'm never going to see him again. He's going to leave me here. He should leave me."

"He wanted to *save* you." The demon laughed. "You can't be saved. You're not worth it."

It was obviously true. She stared at the shadow of Elias, in the world where her body was. She could see Elias's cousin talking to him, obviously urging him to leave. Her companion was by her side, also talking, and the cousin looked back at him, before they both looked at Elias, as if listening to what he was saying. The mafia man, her numbed mind unable to recall his name, laid a hand on the cousin, pulling her back a few steps, even as she shook her head. What was going on? Why were they dawdling? Go already!

And then she saw shadow Elias turn, a needle in his other hand.

"No... don't....!" she tried to say, tried to raise a hand to stop him, but he couldn't hear her, and her hand didn't actually move. She watched him buckle over, the fire burning through his being. She watched the drug tear away at his soul, rending it from his body. Sparks shivered off of him in crackling snaps, making him real to her, burning away the shadow.

"Elias!" she tried to shout, and maybe she actually did that time. Then he collapsed to his knees, the needle still in his arm, his head flopping forward. Somehow she moved, her body obeying her soul as she slid to the ground before him to grip his shoulders. His head wavered drunkenly as he raised it, smiling at her. "Why did you do that? What are you doing!?" she screeched.

"I'm staying with you," he said, simply, continuing to smile as he leaned forward to set his head against her shoulder.

"What?" she squeaked, her voice failing her as the drug worked harder to consume her. "You can't. You don't have to...why would you...?"

She knew the answer to all of those questions. Still, it shocked her as he whispered, "Because you are where my life is."

"But this...this isn't a folktale. No one makes grand sacrifices for love..."

"We're both too old for this bullshit," he answered, the first cuss word she had ever heard from his mouth. Then he took her face in his hands and kissed her, and kissed her well. And she could feel it. Through the numbness, it was real and alive and everything she had ever wanted. How many times had he kissed her like this? What would it take for her to finally learn?

Then he was torn away from her, yanked back by someone gripping his hair.

"No!" she shouted, but she didn't have the strength to hold on to him.

The demon dragged him across the floor, flinging him hard onto a newly emptied mattress. Elias didn't resist, the drug in his system making him helpless and insensate. The demon chuckled while he leaned over his new prize, grabbing his face in one of his long-fingered hands, the joints wrapping around his head as it lifted it up.

"No, stop!" Margaret tried to say, but the demon ignored her, licking Elias's face before plunging into his mouth, kissing and eating at the same time. As the creature sucked, the flames in the walls warped and twisted impossibly, a war scene played out within. Elias killing viciously in a battle, gunfire all around him. Elias flinging magic, then trying to hold a shield against the bullets, but he faltered. The gunfire tore down those around him, the ones he failed to protect. A man screaming in German rushed him and Elias dropped the shield in time to flip his assailant over a shoulder, onto the ground amongst the dead. With blind fury, Elias pummeled his enemy in the face. He didn't stop when blood splattered him. He didn't stop at the loud crunch of bone. He didn't stop, but pounded and pounded, all the while screaming himself hoarse. "I am the Wizard of Death!" the warring Elias screamed madly into the sky.

She wanted to stand up and go to him, to stop the raping of his soul. She tried, but her body wouldn't obey. She wasn't even sure how she had moved before. Then, two pairs of hands gripped her, lifting her up to her feet. Unable to see past the shadows, she had no other choice but to trust those hands to hold her steady.

"Stop it!" she shouted. The demon turned to face her, his ecstatic face turning cruel. The forms on the bed stirred, some turning to look as before. Not having any of it, the demon moved to grip her face, bringing it closer to his own.

"It is too late to care, you are mine, given willingly," he said, and ran another finger along her other cheek, hooking the needle point into her unfeeling skin, to draw her closer. "You will receive what you have always wanted. I will never let you go again. I was too careless and arrogant before, thinking you would never dare leave me."

Margaret thought about all the things she had done to buy the privilege of putting herself in this monster's power.

"You made me pay you for this," she whispered out loud, her thoughts no longer in her head but displayed for him to see, dancing in the flames. For the first time, she could see them too, because she cared to.

"Not anymore," he assured. "I will keep you here with me every moment of your very, very long life. All for free. Aren't I generous?"

"You took pleasure in watching me...in making me do..." The visions of all she had done taunted her in the fires.

"Everything you deserved, yes. It was a delight." His face was too close, his breath foul as he forced a kiss on her. Normally, she wouldn't resist, because often allowing him to do these things meant she could score a second syringe, but now...

"No." She pushed away. Her cheek tore on his talon, but she couldn't feel it. She didn't like this anymore, not feeling anything.

"No pain, no pleasure, no life at all," he promised.

"You only gave me pain or nothing!" she shouted at him. "I don't want to feel nothing anymore!"

The demon smiled. "Too bad."

She managed to push past him, the hands there to support her, following where she wanted to go. It was a stumbling mess, but she made it to Elias's side. He was looking up at the wall, his body frozen stiff, in the throes of the drug. She tried to turn his face away. "Elias. Elias, look at me. Look at me, please."

"Raymond," Elias moaned out, keeping his eyes on the wall. Blinking, Margaret lifted her gaze. The scene in these flames hadn't changed, it was still the scene of Elias straddling the corpse as he punished it, doused in blood. He wasn't stopping of his own accord but was being forced to stop by the young Raymond. The young man discarded his gun and tried to restrain Elias, grappling his arms from behind. Elias fought him briefly, but Raymond had all the leverage, pulling him off the body and to his feet before spinning him around and holding him hard. Elias squirmed in his embrace, fighting for the sake of it and nothing more, but after a few moments, he collapsed to his knees amongst the bodies of his friends. Only Raymond kept his feet, shouting silently, pulling Elias away to run.

"Raymond," Margaret said as well.

"Yes," his lilting voice answered. Margaret jumped. *"I am here, Sistah."*

"Where?" she asked, barely whispering it. She couldn't see him.

"You called to me, and I came." The flames in the wall shifted and shaped the young soldier again.

"Called you?" She blinked, understanding it was true. "You're a ghost."

"You're just a dream," Elias croaked out, his eyes still on Raymond.

Margaret turned to look around the room. All of the flames held ghosts. Ghosts of the past, being torn away and consumed by the demon, or rather, bad memories that haunted every individual in the demon's clutches. They were being torn away with pieces of their souls, so the sad junkies didn't have to feel them anymore. The demon took their life force with it.

"Milking them like cows, until they're milked out, and then consuming them whole," she muttered. She glanced at the pair of blackened chairs. The demon had returned to his, watching, amused as she struggled against his pull on her life and magic through the drug inside her.

And in the distance, the baby cried.

"Come, I will silence it," the demon offered, with a knowing smirk. In his hand, he held out another syringe already prepared. She stared at it. "Let me shut that brat up again."

"My baby?" Margaret willingly listened, for the first time, to the crying of the baby.

Her baby.

"Come to me, baby," she said.

Abruptly the crying grew louder as a spark of light burst into the space. The little light, pure and white, darted around blindly, and the crying became words.

"Where are you? Where are you, Mommy?"

"I'm here! I'm here, baby," Margaret called out. "Come to me."

With glee, the light darted to Margaret's open arms. "I'm sorry, Mommy! I'm sorry!"

Margaret thought she would laugh through her tears. "Sorry? Why are you sorry, baby?"

"I got lost, Mommy! I wasn't able to be born. I love you, Mommy!"

"I love you, too, my baby."

There was a roar, and Margaret staggered to her feet, her baby's light in her arms. The demon raged. It stormed toward her, murder in its eyes. It would destroy them both.

"Raymond! Help me!" she called.

The demon staggered as the ghost slammed into him, ramming the butt of his rifle into the creature's side. The demon tried to bat him back, but the quick soldier ducked before striking another blow, using the rifle as a club.

"Help me!" Margaret shouted as she dropped down beside Elias to try to get him onto his feet. She only had her one arm, though, as she didn't dare let go of her baby.

"Call them again, Margaret," Elias said, as he struggled up. "Mean it. Call the ghosts. It's your Talent. Give them direction."

Margaret had no idea what he meant, but she trusted and that was enough. "Come to me! Help me!"

A wave of sound burst from Margaret like a sonic wave, rippling over the forms and flames. The flames dimmed in the walls before bursting hotter and brighter than before. Forms climbed from them, spilling out. Twisted, tormented souls set free from their imprisonment. Raymond was flung back just in time for the other ghosts to crawl up and over the demon, who screamed, trying to tear the remnants away and failing.

Margaret stared in fascinated horror as he disintegrated into tar-like goop, the ghosts piling on top before melting into the goo themselves. Over and over again, they came, muffling the demon's cries with their own screams of anger and torment.

Without her realizing it, Elias wrapped himself around her, his arms holding on tight, trying to both balance and protect at the same time.

"We need to get out of here," he said.

"Out?" Margaret couldn't understand what he could mean. Out of where? This was a drug high, a living nightmare.

"My Lady!" Elias called out, his voice echoing with power.

"Dammit, Elias!" another voice shouted. It sounded like his cousin.

He laughed, and a string made of pure gold light unfurled from his chest, extending through the flame like a lifeline. Gripping Margaret tight in one arm, he clasped the thread with his other hand. Then her vision filled with golden light.

CHAPTER 10

"DO YOU WANT SOMETHING ELSE TO DRINK?" ELIAS'S COUSIN, RUNE, asked her.

"Um, no," Margaret answered, staring down at the drink before her.

"I think she's still trying to process what happened," Elias explained. He sat on the stool beside her at the island of his kitchen. All of them nursed drinks from his private stash.

"*I'm* still trying to process what happened," St. Benedict said, before tipping his glass into his mouth, the mostly ice clinking as he did so.

"I told you, I pulled them through a veil between worlds," Rune stated, exasperated.

"No, you didn't. You can't pull someone out of a drug high," the Saint argued.

"How else would you explain it? What do you want from me?" she pushed back, throwing her hands up.

"A reasonable explanation would be nice," he repeated.

"It wasn't just a drug high," Elias cut in. "The demon created a pocket world, trapping our souls there while our bodies co-existed here. We were literally in two places at once. What Rune did was pull us back from there."

"Well, it got really freaky when we saw you being dragged across the floor by nothing. And then she," St. Benedict pointed at Margaret, "started flailing around. You both look like hell, and I still think we should take you to the hospital right now and get you detoxed." The Saint picked up a peanut from a bowl sitting on the counter, cracking the shell with a nice snap.

"We'll be fine with some rest," Elias assured as he took a sip of his drink.

"You don't look fine. You look like you've literally aged twenty years," St. Benedict said, then jabbed a finger at the no-longer-smashed mirror hanging over Elias's bed, visible from their seats. "Look for yourself."

They did. Reflected in the mirror was a man in his mid to late fifties, silver streaks through his dark hair. Next to him was a woman about the same age. Both looked like they had been very ill, with a sickly pallor and bags under their eyes.

"Could be worse," Elias commented with a shrug.

"Why couldn't you cross back yourself?" Rune asked. "No, wait. What I really want to know is, did you know I would be able to pull you back out like that?"

"No, I didn't," Elias admitted, grinning.

Rune picked up a towel from his stove and swatted it in Elias's direction. "Don't smile at me. I'm very, very angry at you right now."

"How old are you?" Margaret asked, finally looking up, directing the question pointedly at Rune. The suddenness made everyone stop their banter.

"Um, twenty-six. Closer to twenty-seven," Rune answered. That earned her a furrowed brow from Margaret. "How old are you?"

"Sixty-eight."

"Oh!" Rune's eyebrows shot to the ceiling. "Oh...you look good for your age."

Margaret looked up at the mirror again over the bar. "No, I don't."

"She's a Magi, like us," Elias said.

Rune nodded. "No, no, I get it, you said earlier...I mean, I still have a hard time understanding this Magi thing. Or that you're almost bicentennial."

Elias shrugged.

"Why not? Magic cheats," St. Benedict said, cracking another peanut. Rune pointedly put an empty bowl next to him. He stared at it a moment, then swiped up his small pile of shells and dropped them in. "Yes, dear."

Margaret double blinked, wondering, but not daring to ask if these two were a couple. They certainly acted like it. Instead, she focused on the conversation. "Elias. I need you to finish explaining."

"You have more questions?"

"Yes. I still don't know what you... what *we* are. You aren't just a wizard. Magic folk aren't any different than anyone else, they live normal lives and die normal deaths, and then there's you, living two hundred plus years. Will she?" Margaret countered, giving him an appraising, don't-try-to-con-a-con look as she nodded at Rune, still standing across the counter.

He nodded in return. A different, more somber looked passed over the Saint's face. So apparently, he understood what a Magi was.

"Will I?" Margaret asked.

Elias sighed, clearly recognizing he was trapped. "You are a Magi."

Margaret fixed him with a stare until he continued. "You're right, we are not human. And we don't have normal life spans."

"Then what am I?" she pressed. "What *is* a Magi?"

"I can only really explain in comparison to other hominals." He gripped his drink in his hand, starting and stopping a couple of times, but she waited patiently. "Hominals have souls, right? And in regards to souls...We don't know much about them. We also don't really know how or why magic works, or how hominals or any beings with souls and magic work together, but there is some connection."

"Alright, that's what we don't know, what do we know?" Margaret pressed.

"Magi's souls are made of only magic. Though that's not completely correct either. Our life source, whatever combination of energies that allows us to exist, is what we are made of. It is why we are so powerful. We can create great works of magic, world-changing, world-shattering magic."

"But it will also kill us," Margaret concluded.

He nodded. "The more you drain, the faster you die. It is the most common way for our kind to pass. I'm pretty sure that's what killed my great aunt." A look passed between himself and his cousin. Rune turned away, tears pressing in her eyes, and her maybe-boyfriend grasped her hand as they waited for it to pass.

It was the first time Elias had mentioned a great aunt, but Margaret stowed away the questions about her for later. She needed to understand this now.

"Are *we* related then?" she asked.

Elias chuckled. "There are Magi families, but it's not necessarily a guarantee. Many of us have normal, hominal children, and Magi can appear in families that have never had them before. We aren't sure exactly how it occurs. Magical souls choosing to be born? It seems to have an evolutionary basis of some sort."

"What do you mean?" St. Benedict asked. Apparently, he didn't know everything.

"Whenever a new one of us is born, it creates a new form of magic. All magic evolves from a Magi. Other beings who can wield magic, they can only do what another Magi has created. We each have a… a great working. A great magic that we alone create, and others perpetuate."

"We are… gods?" Margaret grasped.

He laughed. "No. I wouldn't call us gods. Just really magic-upped beings."

"What was your great working?" his cousin asked. So, she didn't know everything either. Margaret was starting to understand Elias more. It wasn't just her he kept his secrets from. Maybe she, in fact, knew more than most.

Elias forced a weak smile. "That's private."

"And when we use our magic, we grow older?" Rune asked this time, surprised.

"Yes, because it's our life force. It always regenerates, but sustained spells and the like can keep one of us perpetually older."

"Like Maddie," Rune said softly.

Elias nodded. "Some of us stretch ourselves too thin for too long."

"Aging is not a curse," Margaret said, giving the girl a sour look.

"No, it's not," Elias agreed, softening her sour with his sweet smile. "It's beautiful, and using our magic is beautiful."

Margaret felt her cheeks pink and she looked down, unable to suppress a return smile.

Elias continued. "And yes, it is why that demon wanted you. A very generous and self-sustaining food supply, as long as you stayed."

"I'm glad we could help," Rune said. Reaching forward, she patted Margaret's hand. "I'm glad we could find you. I wasn't too sure I could do it."

Margaret withdrew her hand quickly. Rune blinked in surprise but settled back, accepting she had crossed a bridge too far.

"Um, well, I gotta check on things at the bar, or Alf will freak out. Do you need anything else before we go?" Rune asked, indicating to St. Benedict with her eyes to move toward the door.

"Thank you, no. We're okay now," Elias said and got up to hug his cousin.

Margaret felt a familiar pang of jealousy, until St. Benedict stuck his hand out to her to shake, distracting her. "Nice to meet you," he said, with a charming smile that killed her sour feelings long enough for her to concede, shaking his hand.

Then they were gone.

"Well, not exactly how I wanted you to meet my cousin, but I guess it could have gone worse," Elias said, once the door was shut. She looked up at him as he approached her side, taking a finger to trace a strand of her hair back behind her ear. He shrugged. "Don't worry. I have an uncle I'm somewhat close to as well. We'll do a better introduction then."

Margaret looked away and picked up her drink.

"Margaret?" he asked softly, just before it reached her mouth. She knew what he was asking with that one word.

"You said you didn't do forever," she answered and took a sip that turned into a gulp once the sweetness of the rum and coke hit her tongue.

"I did."

"What happened?"

He took up his own drink, a Manhattan, an old man's drink. "I changed my mind."

"That's it? You changed your mind? And I'm supposed to believe that is because I'm special? More special than any other person you've ever been with? That it's all magic and puppies and happiness."

"Yes. You are." He turned around to lean back against the counter, keeping the same almost-too-close distance. She felt his heat. She would feel more if she just dared bridge the gap.

"I don't see how." She took a deep breath.

"Then I'll spend every day of my life showing you," he said.

"Romantic crap," she muttered, but it was undercut by her blush and the smile that bubbled up in spite of herself. Over Elias's shoulder, a little light danced. Margaret's face fell a little as she watched her baby's light feather unnoticed through his hair, playing. Then she screwed up her face and courage. She knew what she had to say, and she knew what it would mean. It would mean she would lose him anyway, but she wasn't going to stop.

"I want children," she said, looking at the refrigerator so she wouldn't lose her nerve when he reacted. "I have a baby that needs to be born. I don't know how, but I know it's what I want more than anything."

"Alright."

She paused, lifting her drink to her lips, not daring to look at him. Instead, she questioned, "Alright?"

"Yes. Alright."

"You don't want to have children."

He set his glass down. "No. I do. I want lots of children. I always have. But I believed it would be a mistake. That living life would be a mistake. Yet, I have wondered over the last few years if that wasn't me just being a coward. And then I met you." He turned her chin toward him with gentle fingers. "It isn't the same. I'm not going to be starting over with someone who is just starting out. I'll be starting over with someone who is also starting over. We can figure it out together."

Margaret felt her face harden. "I don't believe you." Her heart pounded as she took a drink, a deep, long, glass-emptying drink, hoping the burn inside would give her the courage that she always assumed it would.

"How can I prove myself to you, my Love?" Elias asked, undeterred. Always undeterred.

She shot him a glare. "Marry me," she demanded. "Because I want that too. I'm not having a bastard child, and you said you didn't want to get married, so how can..."

"Tonight?"

She double blinked. "Really?"

"Is there any reason to wait?"

"You would marry me?"

He took her hand and pulled her to her feet, kissing the palm of her hand. She went willingly.

"Yes!" he growled and laughed, pulling her closer with obvious intent.

They kissed each other eagerly until he stole Margaret's breath. She felt his heartbeat thunder under her hands and without much more thought about it she began to pull up on his sweatshirt.

That broke the kiss as it cleared his head. "Consummation first? I thought you were an old-fashioned girl?" he jibbed, as his undershirt went with the sweatshirt, leaving his leaned muscled frame exposed to the air and Margaret's gaze.

"You're not getting married in a sweatshirt and jeans," she replied, plucking at the top button of his jeans. "Besides, I want to be sure of what I am getting. You might have some more secrets you're hiding from me." Then she was able to open the top and stared at what was there.

"Not much of a secret. I do believe you've already seen me naked."

"I wasn't really looking," she countered, her cheeks blushing.

"Well?"

"Yeah, I guess that will do."

He growled deep in his throat as he swept her up in his arms, carrying her into their bedroom. She laughed and clung on all the way as he passed through the door, but the laughter stopped as abruptly as it began.

"What's wrong?" he asked.

"But...I destroyed it..." Margaret dropped her feet to stand, and Elias set her down as she continued to stare at the star-covered dress, hanging majestically in the closet as new and clean and wonderful as when he'd bought it for her. She had to reach out to touch the skirt to believe it was real. Elias came up behind her, kissing the place where her shoulder met her neck. She fingered the cloth gently. "Magic?"

"Naturally," he whispered, wrapping his arms around her and rocking her gently. "I want you to be wed in it."

Margaret bit her lip. "But what if...What if we change our minds? You said we will both live a long time... What if we get sick of each other?"

"Then we take a break until we're ready to fall in love again and again."

She smiled at that thought. "That sounds like something to look forward to."

"It does, doesn't it?"

Margaret nibbled her lower lip a moment. "I have one last demand."

"Name it."

"I want to go back to school."

"School?"

"All of it. I want to get every degree. And then I want to finish Raymond's work upstairs."

"As you wish, my Love," Elias agreed.

"Good," Margaret said. Then she turned and hugged him hard. "Do you think this will work? Can the Wizard of Death and the Crone have a happily ever after?"

"I think it's worth a try."

"So do I."

EPILOGUE

"WELL, THAT WAS ROMANTIC," ST. BENEDICT SAID AS HE FINISHED TYING his scarf.

"Sure, I guess," Rune said, looking back at the window above. The light went out, and the two figures on the street looked at each other, a knowing smile passed between them. "But do you think it was necessary? Risking his life like that..."

St. Benedict contemplated the question a moment as snow began to dance through the air. "It can be impossible to convince someone to save themselves. When that happens, all you can do is sit with them...I'm sure there's a more poetic way to say that."

"You mean like, sometimes to save someone from hell, you have to go to hell? No, that doesn't sound right."

"It sounds better than what I said," he admitted, offering his arm to her to take. "But you get the idea."

She linked her arm with his but didn't let the idea go as they began to stroll down the wetted street. "Then there was someone?" she said softly to herself.

"Excuse me?"

"You just sound like you're speaking from experience."

"I am."

"And did you save them?"

His expression grew somber. "No. They saved me."

Rune didn't want to hear any more. She had a good idea who "they" were and she didn't want to hear about his wife again. She didn't want to admit it, but she was jealous of a woman who was both alive and dead, a woman who was no longer a part of his life and yet bound him away from the possibility of ever sharing more of it with Rune. It was petty, she knew, but...but he didn't leave it there in the silence.

"The point of hell is to strip away everything you are. They take everything from you, every defense, every lie that you set your identity on. It all gets ripped from you. Even the truths you thought were so very concrete crumble. They take it all. I remember their laughter." He had stopped walking, not because he meant to stop, but as if momentum was too hard to achieve, weighed down by memories he had never shared with her before. Memories too similar to her own, but she pushed them back into their box in her mind.

Instead, she squeezed his arm, wanting to slip into his embrace, but she could never risk doing that. He couldn't belong to her like that.

Then he raised his head to look at her with haunted eyes that saw and showed so much. "I'm sorry. This must be torture for you..." he whispered.

She tried to lick her dry lips with her dry tongue. "No, it's okay."

Something shone in his eyes as he searched her face. "Is it?"

"Of course," Rune smiled over her own pain. While it wasn't a shared pain exactly, it was one they both understood too well, that place he had called hell. "We're friends. You can tell me anything. I won't judge you."

St. Benedict nodded, swallowing. After a heartbeat, he found his smile again, and they continued on to where his car was parked down the block. Rune had gotten used to the vehicle sensing St. Benedict's approach before unlocking itself and flipping on the internal light, yet her magical-based mind still found it marvelous. No spell in her mind would automatically turn on the seat warmers, that was for sure.

"What still kind of shocks me is how she lived so many decades, never having a clue what she really was," Rune said as she clicked her seatbelt in place, the car already growling to life.

"Really? How is it that strange? You didn't know *you* were a Magi until a few months ago, and that was only after Elias explained it to you, right?" St. Benedict said, turning around in the driver's seat to back up out of his spot. When Rune didn't respond, he paused and turned forward again to glance at her.

Rune gave him a guilty side glance. "That's not exactly true."

St. Benedict jerked his head back. "What?"

Rune tucked her arms around herself. "I've always known what I was. Maddie told me when I was a kid."

"But... you were so surprised when Elias..." He shook his head. "When I met you last year, you kept saying you were just a Talent."

"Yes, it was a lot better than admitting the truth to anyone. Look, I'm not saying I entirely understood what being a Magi meant, and there was a time when my magic was...stuck. Like, I rejected it so hard that I... kept myself from my ability to fully use it. Now, years later, I'm trying to figure it all out. But as a kid, with parents like mine and their friends and all of that, Justin, you know..." Invoking her ex-husband's name sent a shiver down her spine. She shouldn't have brought him up. Or any of this. "I mean, what can I really say after a lifetime of sabotaging myself?"

She glanced up and saw the pity in his eyes, which was worse than censure or judgment. So, to break it up, she slapped her hands on her thighs with a little bounce.

"So, there you are. I lied. What are you going to do about it, Mr. Saint of Liars?" she teased, trying to claw her way back to the cheer they shared when they had left Elias's apartment.

"Nothing," he said, his voice filling with laughter. "We just can't call you the Finder of Truth now."

"I think I like the Finder of the Lucky Devil better," she replied, tossing her hair with a mock-heroic swish.

"I think I do, too," he answered.

AN EXCERPT FROM

THE FINDER OF THE LUCKY DEVIL

CHAPTER 1

SIX YEARS LATER...

THE BAR WAS OVERCROWDED. AFTER THE THIRD TRAY OF GLASSES crashed to the floor, Rune seriously considered the legal ramifications of whipping out her great aunt's old shotgun and clearing the room.

It all started when the bachelorette party exploded out of the backroom and into the quieter sanctuary of the Lounge Bar. Alf, the bar's general manager, made her book the Quintet of Stupid, reminding her that the mortgage bill was coming due in less than a week. Not that she needed reminding. Grumbling under her breath about selling him to the lollipop guild, she had confirmed the date and time. The way the maid of honor had been talking, one would think they were having an entire party of twenty or more people. Rune was irritated beyond belief when they showed up with only five, all wearing bedazzled shirts designating them as princess bride, maid of dishonor, the rebel bridesmaid, the fat bridesmaid, and the replacement bridesmaid.

"Exactly, how much are they going to drink if they're already drunk?" Rune grumbled under her breath at Alf, after she had led the small party to their private room in the back.

"They've prepaid the room and the drinks, so stop your bitching." Alf slapped his damp shoulder towel onto the bar to swipe peanut shells into an empty trash bin that floated up on its own next to him. "And where are all the bottle openers?"

Rune didn't need to look; she never did. She just reached back behind herself and swiped the green one from next to the cash register to hand to the little man. Though Alf only reached about mid-waist, he gave her an intimidating glare. He was a dwarf, but not *that* kind of dwarf, and he would be the first to kneecap anyone for making that mistake.

"Hey Alf, the bathroom cleaning spell is wearing off in the men's bathroom," one of the regulars, a vampire named Morlock, informed them as he swiped up the shot and blood chaser waiting for him. "Smells like something died in there."

"Now if you could just do some actual magic, and not just find things," Alf said at Rune.

"You can't do magic? Whoa, wait, weren't you Maddie's apprentice?" Morlock asked, tapping his shot glass on the bar for another hit.

"If she could, do you think I would be heading off to manually clean a bathroom?" Alf groused as he hopped down from his literal soapbox.

Rune made a face at her bar manager when his back was turned and opened the register with a quick, muttered spell word. She touched one finger to the crystal set at the top to activate the "unlock" magic. It wasn't that she couldn't do magic. She had a magical Talent, it was just for Finding things, which was a pretty passive, quiet magic. She sighed to herself, knowing they were going to have to pay for someone to recast the "auto cleaning" spell for them, and that was going to be pricey.

Rune tucked the party deposit under the tray in the register, annoyed that they were so late with it. She should have just given the room away, but they kept promising to bring it in, only to do so the night of the party. Yet, she knew Alf was right about booking the bridal party despite the risk. It irked her just the same. While the deposit went a long way, Rune was still $2500 short on the mortgage. Getting the rest of the fee would be its own nightmare and far too late to help with this month.

"If we hadn't booked it out, we could have opened it up for more game patrons," Rune argued to herself, but she wasn't buying it.

The Lounge Bar was moderately attended for a Wednesday night, mostly working couples looking to unwind in the dimmer, calmer atmosphere. By contrast, the Main Bar was overly full as the Chicago Cubs were playing the New York Mets. From the sounds in the next room, Chicago was doing pretty well. That was when the first tray of glasses crashed in the Main Bar. Alf hurried past from the bathrooms to see what happened, leaving Rune alone to run the Lounge.

"Hey, Rune!"

She looked over her shoulder at the centaur sitting at his usual place at the end of the old stained bar. He was slovenly dressed in a disheveled business jacket, with his tie mostly undone around his neck and his sleeves rolled up in a way that Rune didn't think the suit was ever designed for. He wore a matching, gray, formal apron, cut much like a horse blanket, sitting askew across his horse-like body. Rune thought the idea of a formal apron was silly looking but dared not say that to a centaur. He smiled at her warmly, the smile cracking across his brown face and enviably perfect white teeth. His mane and tail were done up in dreadlocks, the neatness of his hair making an odd counter to his rumpled clothes.

Rune pushed off the back wall and made her way unhurriedly down the bar, smiling. All the other patrons seemed satisfied enough at the moment, so she grabbed up a bottle of ginger ale and cracked it open to drink and enjoy with her friend.

"Are you sure you need another, Franklin?" she asked, teasingly, trying not to sound too motherly, while the effervescent bubbles burned up her nose.

"No, but I'm sure you need one. Have a drink with me, Rune." He folded both his arms onto the bar and leaned as far forward as he dared, making the whole bar creak as he gave it his weight. Franklin was a regular customer and the large centaur knew his limits. Even when he didn't, he never caused a scene.

"I can't have a drink with you, Frankie. Not tonight. Things are a bit on edge. Baseball next door," Rune said politely enough, as she pulled him another beer from the tap, an IPA from Wisconsin. She set the tall glass on a cardboard coaster and slid the whole thing toward his big meaty hands. Instead of the beer, he caught her hand, folding her fingers over the top of his larger, longer ones, pinning the tips with his thumb gently but firmly.

"Go out on a date with me, then," Franklin said, doubling down and tugging her a bit closer, to bring her knuckles up so that his breath rolled over them as he spoke.

"Sorry, but no. I'm not your type," she said, then amended, "I don't mean that how it sounds...which just makes it sound worse, I know." This was not the first time Franklin had asked this question but it didn't seem to stop him when he'd had a few. Rune just never could figure out how to put him off for good without hurting his feelings. He loosened his grip on her fingers just enough for her to snatch them away before he could lay a big, old, sloppy, wet kiss on them. Instead, he groaned melodramatically.

"Oh Rune, please. What do I have to do?"

"Stop being a cliché when a girl tells you no?" she quipped.

"I just want a real woman and you are really a woman," he said, following his own drunken logic.

"You mean all size twelve of me?" she threw back at him.

Rune was feeling a bit cheeky that night. Being a size twelve didn't bother her much; in her opinion, it was in all the right places. That night she wore one of her taper-cut blouses, her dark brown one that emphasized her bust, cinching her much smaller middle before flaring out again at her hips. She had taken to wearing skinny jeans again after a long stint in boot cut. Skinny jeans tucked better into the knee-high brown boots that she favored at the moment. She loved earth tones and real clothes made from cotton, leather, and metal, having spent too much of her previous life in synthetics. Apparently, Franklin loved it too.

"Girl, what hot-blooded male doesn't want a woman of substance?" Franklin asked, and she flashed him a shameless smile. Luckily for her, she got another hail from back down the bar allowing her to make a smooth, tasteful escape.

"To be continued. I'll be right back, Franklin."

"Let them wait. Come on. Why don't you ever say yes?"

"Franklin, you're a nice enough guy, but I am just not interested, really." Rune hoped this came off as letting him down gently but firmly.

"What? What is it, Rune? What is wrong with me? I'll change, I promise. I'm not like those other males who can't be changed. I'll change for you all day long! I promise," he begged, sliding his arms across the bar so that he was lying on it, the picture of dejection.

"Sounds like a lot of work. It's easier to give up on dating all together. It just doesn't work out for me," she laughed. "You know the saying right? I got baggage you don't want."

"Rune, you should have more confidence in yourself," Franklin said as if he thought he was being helpful.

Rune faltered and then forced her smile again. "Sorry, but I'm feeling the pressure from needing to serve those other patrons. I'll be back, I promise." As she turned, she saw Alf intercept them, after giving her a dirty look.

"What kind of guys do you go for then?" another voice asked.

Normally, Rune would have noticed the newcomer when he slid up next to her on the other side of the bar. It was an instinct developed by years of looking over her shoulder, but this gentleman had appeared almost like magic, which was likely to be more literal than metaphorical. Rune still found it unsettling and irritating; though maybe not as strange as it would have been at one of the more hominal-only bars in the city.

What did unsettle her was how he stared directly at her with intense green eyes rimmed with blue. Being the focus of his stare made her trip, trapped in his gaze, as if she was locking eyes with a wolf. He was dressed in a fine suit, charcoal gray and three-piece, with a matching fedora and a stench of money about him. He was also unfairly handsome, with an angular face and cheekbones that could cut glass. The edges of his hat showed dark hair, and the cut of his suit suggested a man who did a lot of swimming; all lithe strength without the bulk from weight-lifting. She would even bet he had suspenders on, though that thought only lived in her imagination. Rune loved men in suspenders.

Then that arresting gaze softened so quickly, Rune wondered if she had misinterpreted what she had seen. He smiled broadly, as the wolf faded back and he gave her a charming wink that warmed her insides against her will.

"Clever like a jackrabbit," she muttered under her breath. He blinked and cocked his head to the side.

"Sorry?" he asked, blinking twice more before leaning on the bartop and wrapping his hands around the opposite elbows.

"Uh, it's just a saying of my great aunt's. The charming ones are by far more dangerous than the handsome ones; just ask anyone who went up against the jackrabbit," she explained, rubbing at the top of the bar with a damp cloth to cover up her embarrassment at being overheard. She kicked at the magically sentient garbage can that tapped eagerly at her legs, like a dog looking for crumbs.

"Then which am I? Charming or handsome?" the jackrabbit man asked, a wicked, knowing gleam in his eye that now looked wolfish again.

"Hmm, neither," Rune said like a smartass with a hint of flirt.

"What kind of guys do you like then, Rune?" Franklin interjected, obviously concerned that she was paying attention to another male.

"I suppose someone who's interested in starting a conversation with me that doesn't include my dating preferences. Maybe a conversation about the feminine mystique or the nuances of British Parliamentary procedure. You know, the usual, because we're an advanced society and all," Rune said in a syrupy-sweet voice accompanied by an acrid smile.

"Ah, a progressive woman I see. That's refreshing in a bar," the mystery man said.

"And why is that?" Rune asked, drawn in, in spite of herself.

"I would think it would be more advantageous to you to play dumb and smile a lot to increase your tip count. Isn't that the usual, smart business plan for a female bartender?" he asked so pleasantly that it almost took away the edge of his words.

"Do you often get away with saying rude, sexist things by being dark, handsome, and mysterious?" she shot back, her eyes and her smile widening like a cat before she pounced. This was getting fun.

"Ah, so I am handsome then?" he countered, smirking even harder, as if he won.

Both males stared at her, but it was the stranger who captured Rune's gaze again. Under his unwavering smile, she felt her cheeks flush bright pink, like she was in high school. Franklin looked back and forth between them, not liking that their gazes were locked or what it might mean.

"Hey, Rune. Is this guy bothering you?" Franklin asked, using the old cliché instead of coming up with something original to say. It was enough, because the stranger broke their connection to smile at Franklin as some sort of gear shifted between himself and Rune.

"I'll have a vodka tonic and another beer for my new friend here," he said inclining his head toward Franklin, "and whatever you want for yourself. I have some more questions for you about dark, handsome, mysterious men. And also I have..." he reached into his jacket's front pocket. Before Rune could see what was inside, Franklin shoved himself up to his hooves.

"None for me, thanks. I need to piss like a racehorse," Franklin said, digging up another bad taste cliché, obviously irritated as he pushed away from the bar, unsteady on his hooves.

"Franklin, are you alright?" Rune asked, feeling unsure about his sudden departure. He waved her off.

"I'll see you tomorrow, Rune. I should be getting home," he said and clomped his way to the front in a mostly straight line.

"Uh, yeah, see you later, Franklin," Rune called after him, trying to sound cheerfully nonchalant to mask her worry.

He paused at the sound of her voice, but his shoulders slumped noticeably when he heard her words. She received a backward wave as he trotted out the door, instead of to the restrooms.

"Ah, geez," she said to herself under her breath and opened the cooler in front of her to toss the ice in irritation. "Sorry, what was it you ordered again?" she asked as she tried to refocus and push down the sad feeling in her stomach. Before the stranger could speak, one of the Back Bar bartenders came up behind Rune, making her jump a little.

"Hey Boss, sorry. I think we're out of the cherry liquor and I can't find any more in the back."

Rune blinked at her as if she couldn't comprehend what she was looking at before nodding. "Cherry liquor? For the bridal party from hell?"

"Yeah, they're burning through Tainted Virgins like they're mineral water," the bartender complained.

Rune stepped back and reached up to slide the bottle of cherry liquor off the shelf, and handed it to her bartender. "You're doing a good job, just hang in there," Rune said.

"Wow, I should have you come to my apartment and help me find my lost keys. At this rate I'm going to have to marry a locksmith," she said, bubbly, and then headed toward the Backroom Bar.

"So, you're the owner of this place?" the stranger asked.

"Uh, yeah. Yeah, I am now. The original owner died recently." The knot appeared again, threatening the back of Rune's throat, but she managed to swallow it down. "And she left everything to me! So, here I am, trying to run a bar. Speaking of, you said vodka tonic right?"

"Or a beer if that's easier," he answered.

"It's up to you. I can try either," Rune answered back.

"You know what? Let's just forget about the drink. If you're the owner you might be exactly who I am looking for." He slipped his hand back into the front pocket of his jacket.

And then a woman hailed her just a few feet away at the far edge of the bar. She was so loud that by reflex they both looked at her. It was one of the bridesmaids, drunkenly leaning against the bar, looking like she was a lost contestant from some slutty beauty pageant. The bedazzled shirt that proclaimed her the maid of dishonor was missing a few gems.

"Hey! Bartender!" she shouted too loudly for the easy conversational atmosphere of the Lounge Bar.

"Um, excuse me," Rune said and picked up the rag she had been fiddling with as she walked down the bar to meet the loud woman. "Can I help you?" she asked as she approached, pitching her voice pointedly low in an attempt to get the maid of dishonor to do the same.

"Hi. So, we were supposed to have the devil in our room. What's going on with that?" the maid of dishonor asked, in a pissy tone, completely ignoring Rune's subtle hint to bring it down a notch.

Rune blinked at her for a second and glanced over at Lucky Devil in his booth.

Lucky Devil and the bar that was named for him were both icons of Chicago and the bar's biggest attraction. The Lucky Devil figure sat in the only booth in the whole bar, smiling a wicked smile to the delight of tourists, and was an icon of pride for regular customers as well. He was made out of the same plastic and wood hodgepodge that carousel horses were made of; the inside completely mechanical, except for a couple of magical modifications to prevent rot from various libations of spilled drinks. Yet, the most powerful spell on it was designed for one purpose: to grant wishes.

To look at the Devil himself, one would think he belonged to a lost attraction from Coney Island or a freak show that traveled along back roads. He sat with one arm resting along the back of the booth, alert yet relaxed at the same time. He was jauntily dressed in an old-fashioned yellow suit and bowtie with the standard pointed, black devil beard, and eyebrows arching sharply on his bright Tabasco red skin. Perched on his head was a matching fedora, sitting at an angle amongst black curls, so that one of his horns arched free around the brim. The booth and table were raised up on their own dais so patrons had to step up to sit across from him. Only then could they see his goat furred legs, one black cloven hoof crossed nonchalantly over the knee of the other leg. His other hand rested on the table, a lowball glass gripped in his fist, waiting to be filled. When patrons sat across from him, he stared at them with wicked, smiling eyes and an equally wicked grin that showed a little bit of sharpened tooth.

At that moment, Lucky Devil was entertaining a pair of customers; two young men who were obviously on a first date and seemed to be having a really good one at that. The Latino boy, with long clever hands and a bright, white-toothed smile pulled a tab on the old fashioned cigarette machine that had been repurposed to dispense souvenir coins; each stamped with the bar's logo on one side and a smiling Lucky Devil winking on the other side. The Latino kid had chosen a silver coin, worth about $10, to make his wish with. Apparently, the date was going very well, but not well enough to warrant a $100 coin, which was a combination of gold, silver, and platinum. Most people who purchased those coins never gave them to the Devil to make their wish, but would pocket them as souvenirs to take home. Then there were the jade coins, only twelve ever made, and they always found their way back to the Devil eventually. This kid had no jade coin, nor did he intend to pocket the coin he had purchased. Instead, he slipped back into the booth next to his date, showing him the coin. The other Filipino-looking young man was filling out a slip of paper with a small pencil. They giggled as the Filipino kid folded up the paper, presumably his wish, and tucked it into the front pocket of Lucky Devil's jacket. Then the Latino kid dropped the silver coin into the lowball glass, per the instructions left on the table. Both waited, watching the mechanical devil, eager eyes filled with child-like anticipation. It was so cute that Rune couldn't help but wish she had a camera or imaging crystal to capture it with.

Then the Devil came to life, or so it appeared. The mechanical arm lifted the glass and drank the coin, the mouth dropping open to swallow it. The young couple squealed in delight, grabbing each other's hands in their excitement. Once the Lucky Devil had "emptied" the glass he set it down and gave a merry, menacing chuckle. Eagerly, the Latino kid checked the pocket only to exclaim in shock to his date, that the slip of paper was gone, and that the wish had been "granted".

As she watched, Rune felt the paper appear in the front pocket of her button-up shirt. Though the paper itself didn't weigh much or have much mass, the magic always made her skin tickle when the spell dropped the wish from Lucky Devil's pocket to her own. Or if she didn't have front pockets that day, the spell would redirect to the inside of her bra strap, tingling her skin like the end of a battery.

"Is that the Devil there?" the maid of dishonor demanded.

"Yes, he is." Rune fished the slip of paper out of her front pocket and looked at it. "Hey Liam!" she called over her shoulder. From around the separating wall that led to the Main Bar, a Shiva appeared.

The kid was tall, with nice brown skin and darker hair, dressed in a polo shirt with the Lucky Devil logo over the heart. Rune had to special order the shirt for him with four sleeves, but he wore it religiously when he worked, so she concluded it was worth it. "We need two double-sized frozen Margaritas and some supreme nachos at Lucky Devil's table."

"Put it on his tab?" Liam asked with a wry smile, folding his lower set of arms across his extra-long chest.

Rune nodded and put the piece of paper back into her front pocket. The maid of dishonor eyed both of them with judgmental disgust. Liam's face fell a bit as he turned to head toward the kitchen in the next room.

"Are you listening to me?" the maid of dishonor asked shrilly, making Rune wish a little bit harder that the floor would open up and swallow the woman, complete with licking fire and a nice refreshing sulfur smell. "Hey! Hey! I asked you a question. We're supposed to be in the room with the devil."

"That would be this room." Rune dug deep for friendly professionalism and gestured over to Lucky Devil. The young couple at the table squealed again in delight as their drinks appeared with amazing haste. Liam's four fast hands pulled off that miracle, as well as an order of the bar's famous spicy nachos, probably stolen from another order to pull off the Lucky Devil's trick.

"No, no, I was told there is a devil. We want to take pictures," the maid of dishonor snapped again, pulling Rune's attention away from enjoying the couple's delight.

"Yes, there is. You can come out here and take as many pictures as you want," Rune tried again, her irritation evident in her voice and through her smile.

"Look, this is obviously over your little head. I'd like to talk to your manager," the maid of dishonor declared regally.

Before Rune could say something even more unwise, like something degrading about her customer's intelligence, which was too wordy for good banter, Alf shoved Rune out of the way. Rune gave a little puppy yelp as she went flying behind the bar, landing on the cushy mats that helped with foot soreness. Rune cussed under her breath as she rubbed the spot at mid-thigh that Alf had bumped. For a dwarf, or little person, or whatever, he had a very sharp hip bone.

"I am the general manager. How can I help you, ma'am?" Alf said with a sweet, congenial smile as he stood on the built-in step that had been installed along the bottom of the bar just for him.

"I can't believe we're being treated this way," the maid of dishonor repeated in the exact tone she had used on Rune, and then launched into her litany of woe again.

Rune started to pick herself off of the floor when she looked up to see the charming man, leaning forward on his elbows to look down at her. Quickly, Rune mimed a "bada bump ching" on an invisible drum set. The charming guy's grin cracked fully into a smile. "One of my more graceful moments," Rune added as she pulled herself up.

"I can't believe he bumped you like that. Aren't you his boss?" the stranger asked, nodding his head at Alf, who was working full tilt to soothe the maid of dishonor's hurt feelings.

"Depends on the day, I guess," Rune said. "Do you still want that beer... or was it a vodka tonic? Or gin and tonic? Something tonic. I'm almost 90% sure."

"Vodka tonic," he said, and gave her another wink like he was sharing a secret with her.

"Sure, coming right up, I promise." Rune pulled out the tall glass she needed to mix up the drink.

"I must say he's very spritely for a dwarf," the stranger said, nodding in Alf's direction. That brought Rune up short.

"Excuse me?"

The stranger shifted a little, his grin fading just a bit as he tried to figure out what he had said wrong.

"Alf is not a dwarf. He's a hominal person just like you and me, Buddy. The correct term is little person." Rune set the glass down on the bar.

Sure, she thought of Alf as a dwarf, but that was in her own head and only when she was mad at him. This guy was a stranger.

"Hominal?" the stranger asked. Something about him seemed to tense, though he hadn't moved a muscle. In fact, he seemed just as relaxed as ever, yet Rune couldn't shake the feeling that he was about to spring into action.

"Human being. We serve a lot of different peoples here at the Lucky Devil, but don't go making assumptions about any of them, if you please," Rune said. Alf may not have been

Rune's favorite person in the world, but he was one of her people.

"I meant no disrespect. It's just not a term that comes up often for me, or the term dwarf. Is that a derogatory word or something?" the stranger asked, his head tilting to the side just a little, his hat casting a shadow across part of his face.

"He's not a dragon-killing enthusiast or a really good mining/witch-slaying aficionado from the fairy tales. There is a big difference," she said.

"I apologize for my ignorance," he conceded, taking his hat off so that light shined on him again. He held it against his chest as he bowed his head in apology.

That took the wind out of Rune's sails and she started mixing the drink again.

"I'm sorry. I'm just a little on edge tonight." She shoveled ice into the glass.

"Why is that?"

Rune eyed him a moment with a soft smile as she set the glass onto the bar before him and pulled out the pop hose, pushing one of the many buttons on the back to dispense the tonic water.

Before she could answer, Alf appeared like an insistent itch at her elbow. "Jasper and Calvin are here," he growled.

Rune's head shot up to glance sideways over Alf, and sure enough, there was the Tigerman and the hominal man waiting like bad habits at the end of the bar. They were both dressed in slick, high-corporate suits. Rune snorted at the sight of Calvin, who still wore his sunglasses, heedless of being indoors.

"They want their money," Alf said indelicately.

"I got 'til Monday morning. It's only Wednesday. Just ignore them," Rune said in a hushed, confidently defiant voice, just before she flooded the drink with too much tonic water.

"No, you just ignore them." Alf pushed Rune out of the way to swipe up the drink and slap a cloth on the bar to sop the excess liquid spilling to the ground. Rune managed to release her thumb from the button, but the damage was done. Her antics caught Calvin's attention apparently, because he looked at her over his stupid sunglasses. Their eyes met as she glanced nervously back at him, cursing herself silently for looking. Jasper just smiled a toothy grin and continued to munch on the free, shell-on peanuts.

"If you would just attend the Magic Guild summons instead of only paying your dues..." Alf continued to grumble.

Avoiding that sore subject again, Rune apologized to the stranger and handed over the vodka and tonic to Alf, so she could make her way to the corporate thugs waiting for her.

"Aren't those bad for you?" Rune asked Jasper when she approached.

He continued shoveling peanuts, grinning grossly as he snapped them into pieces in his sharp feline teeth. "Lots of things are bad for you," the Tigerman answered.

"Like not making your mortgage payments on time for example." His associate lifted the glasses up off his face to reveal ghostly blue eyes.

"Last I checked my due date is Monday, Calvin," Rune answered innocently, wiping the counter clear of peanut refuse into the eagerly waiting magical bin that had taken up residence at that particular edge, trying to catch the random bits that came its way. "Do you need help finding a calendar?" On reflex, her senses stretched out to pull her toward every available calendar in the room, but Rune ignored it and flashed Calvin a cheeky smile.

That earned her a furrowing of eyebrows and a quiet stare. "Look, we get it, don't we, Mr. Locke? This old place, it's got sentimental value for you. The old lady took you in off the streets after all, but Rune, this does not make good business sense, holding onto this money sink of a place."

"Money pit or sinkhole," Jasper corrected, cracking another peanut.

Calvin shot him a look. "Really? You do this now in front of the client," Calvin said under his breath.

"And yet my bar isn't empty. Funny that," Rune cut in, not wanting to wait for them to resolve their little spat. She eyed the near-empty bowl Jasper was eating out of. "Do you want something to drink with all those peanuts, Jasper?"

"Mr. Locke," the Tigerman corrected narrowing his feline eyes at Rune, which were plenty intimidating.

"We both know…" Calvin started again before his partner cut him off.

"I'll take a Bailey's," Jasper said, "no ice." His partner pursed his lips together and turned his head to his partner in a disapproving manner before swinging it back to Rune and continuing, "We both know that your old boss didn't make her mortgage payments on the proceeds to this place."

"She was a woman of many hobbies." Rune smiled as she brought up a lowball tumbler from under the bar and set it on the counter before fishing around in the little fridge near her foot for the open bottle of Bailey's Irish Cream. "I suppose being a cat person, this makes perfect sense," she said pouring the tumbler a quarter full.

"We're prepared to make you a really good offer, Rune." Calvin pushed the glass away before Rune could pour any more. Jasper growled a little and Calvin gave him a chastising swat on the arm, which completely undermined Jasper's menace. "You can walk away from all this and start a better life."

Rune really didn't know what to say to that, so she just stared him down and hoped it came across as unfazed.

"Or if you want to stay here, a salary can be arranged, but either way, we can take this burden off your hands and make that mortgage just go away."

"I'll have the payment for you on Wednesday morning. Do you want me to come by the office or are you two going to come pick it up again in person?" Rune answered evenly, hugging the Bailey's bottle against her shoulder.

"We're losing our patience, Rune," Calvin warned.

"Do you need help finding that too?" she asked.

That's when the bridal party and a bar fight exploded out of the back room.

ABOUT THE AUTHOR

MEGAN MACKIE IS A WRITER, ACTOR, AND PLAYWRIGHT. SHE STARTED her writing career as an indie author and had such smashing success in her first year with her inaugural book *The Finder of the Lucky Devil*, that she made the transition to traditional publishing. She has become a personality at many cons, recognizable by her iconic leather hat and engaging smile. She has recently joined Bard's Tower, a mobile con bookstore, and has sold her books next to great authors such as Peter David, Melinda Snodgrass, Dan Wells, Claudia Gray, John Jackson Miller, and Jim Butcher, to name a few.

She has written four novels including: T*he Finder of the Lucky Devil, The Saint of Liars, Death and the Crone,* and *Saint Code: Lost* all of which will be re-releasing through eSpec Books. She is also a contributing writer in the role-playing game *Legendlore* soon to be published by Onyx Path Publishing.

Outside of writing she likes to play games: board games, RPGs, and video games. She has a regular Pathfinder group who is working their way through Rapanthuk. She lives in Chicago with her husband and children, dog, three cats, and her mother in the apartment upstairs.